FRIENDLY ADVICE FROM AN ENEMY

Alabeth was stunned by Count Adam Zaleski's uncanny resemblance to the man she had so deeply loved, her late husband, Robert.

But the moment after she left the Count's arms and a dance that left her heart beating wildly, she was even more startled to see Sir Piers Castleton approach her.

She started to turn away, but his voice halted her.

"The handsome, winning ghost you trod a measure with a moment since was no ghost," Piers said in his familiar, infuriatingly arrogant tone. "It was very much a flesh and blood Polish aristocrat with your seduction in mind. Be under no illusion about Zaleski, Alabeth, for it could be your undoing."

Rage flared within Alabeth. How could this man who had so grievously betrayed her husband now presume she would trust a word he said?

Yet could she even trust her own treacherous heart . . . ?

RAKEHELL'S WIDOW

SIGNET Regency Romances You'll Want to Read

RAKEHELL'S *WIDOW*

by Sandra Heath

A SIGNET BOOK

NEW AMERICAN LIBRARY

Copyright© 1984 by Sandra Heath

 SIGNET TRADEMARK REG. U.S. PAT. OFF. AND FOREIGN COUNTRIES
REGISTERED TRADEMARK—MARCA REGISTRADA
HECHO EN CHICAGO, U.S.A.

SIGNET, SIGNET CLASSIC, MENTOR, PLUME, MERIDIAN and
NAL BOOKS are published by New American Library, 1633 Broadway,
New York, New York 10019

First Printing, June, 1984

1 2 3 4 5 6 7 8 9

PRINTED IN THE UNITED STATES OF AMERICA

1

Alabeth drew back the crimson velvet draperies to watch the approach of her father's heavy traveling carriage. Its lamps cast a pale light over the mauve rhododendrons lining the drive and an unseasonal rumble of thunder wandered darkly over the April night sky, followed by a flash of lightning which shone sharply on the coach's polished brasswork and gleaming panels. Why had he decided to pay Charterleigh a visit after all this time? And why make the journey from London to the coast of Kent after a long and tiring day in the House of Lords debating the new peace with France? She knew he hated traveling by night because of the danger of highwaymen, and yet he chose this late hour to visit him. Perplexed, she watched the carriage, its harness jingling and its wheels crunching on the freshly raked gravel. It swung in an arc around the stone fountain before the main entrance of the rambling Tudor house, and then it passed from her sight.

She was thoughtful as she remained by the window. It had been six years now since she had scandalized polite society by jilting the elderly and influential Duke of Treguard at the altar and eloping instead with Robert, Lord Manvers, master of Charterleigh and one of the most notorious rakehells in England. Society had abhorred her actions, finding no mitigating circumstances in the fact that she had been only seventeen and had never wished the arranged match with the Duke in the first place. She had friends who had remained loyal to her, but she had made a great many enemies, many of whom would never forgive her for breaking so many rules. Her father had forgiven

5

her to a certain extent, once he had got over the shame and embarrassment, but he had never once set his seal of approval on her unwelcome marriage by visiting Charter-leigh. She had always been welcome at Wallborough Castle, the family seat in Derbyshire, provided she visited alone, but no single member of her family had ever called upon her. Now she had been a widow for two years, and still those same rules applied—until tonight. Why?

Another vivid flash of lightning pierced the night sky, reflecting clearly in her large green eyes. Hers was a breath-taking beauty, the sort of beauty which even a man like Lord Manvers, who had vowed never to encumber himself with a wife, had been unable to resist. Her hair was dark red, twisted back into a Grecian knot at the back of her head and teased into dainty curls around her face. Her sprigged muslin gown, white picked out with primrose, was a fashionable echo of ancient Greece, with its high waistline and elegant train, reminiscent of the classical lines so much admired now. Slowly she lowered the drap-eries and turned to leave the tapestry-hung room, her cash-mere shawl dragging on the polished wooden floor behind her as she went to greet her father. The sound of his foot-man's cane rapping smartly on the ancient door echoed dully through the house.

The Earl waited in the great hall, a stone-flagged cham-ber with dark paneled walls and a number of suits of armor which always seemed to Alabeth to still contain their long-dead owners. The candles on the walls cast a poor light, but the Earl was standing by the immense stone fireplace where the butler had placed a small oil lamp. Geoffrey Albert Carstairs, eleventh Earl of Wallborough, was a portly man, once considered very good-looking but now rather too round to be called handsome. He did not much care for modern fashions, choosing to still powder his hair and wear colorful coats and buckled shoes, and his face bore a habitually mournful expression that concealed the gruff humor which was the mark of his many speeches in the House.

Her skirts rustled as she approached. "Good evening, Father."

"Beth."

"May I offer you some cognac?" She spoke lightly, but she was nervous as she went to the heavily carved Elizabethan sideboard.

He nodded. "It's good to see you in something other than black for a change."

"My two years of mourning ended in January."

"Two years? Most women settle for one."

"I am not most women."

"By God, that's an irrefutable fact, madam, for how many other women would be so foolish as to ally themselves to a wastrel who then set out deliberately provoking a duel in which he was almost certain to die? Eh? Damn me if I don't think he deserved to snuff it, and that's another irrefutable fact."

"Father, I would prefer not to quarrel with you, but quarrel we will if you persist in speaking ill of Robert in his own house."

"I don't wish to quarrel with you, my dear, but I can't help regretting your past connections with all my heart."

"I loved him, with all *my* heart," she retorted. "And besides, the duel was not of his choosing. It was brought about by the interference and evil influence of Sir Piers Castleton."

The Earl's shrewd eyes moved thoughtfully over her face. "Castleton was his second, not his opponent, 'Beth."

"He was still entirely to blame."

"Well, I admit that Castleton isn't one of my favorite fellows, but I still can't truthfully say that I agree entirely with you. Robert was his own man and nobody's cat's-paw." The Earl accepted the glass of cognac she held out for him. He swirled the amber liquid and sniffed the bouquet. "Some of Robert's contraband stock?" he asked with a smile.

"Smuggling wasn't one of his vices."

"Then he must have been the only gentleman in this part of the country to be so innocent."

"Not everyone in Kent is a smuggler, sir."

"Perhaps not quite, but a more notorious lair of *contrebandiers* would be hard to find. I'll warrant the new peace treaty hasn't been all that well received here, for now there'll be more time for the revenue cutters to do their appointed task."

She smiled. "You may be right."

"What is your opinion of the peace?"

"Well, the thought of continuing with a war which has already lasted eight years isn't cheering, but for all that, I think this particular treaty is a bad thing."

"Ah, so you're a daughter of mine after all," he said with some satisfaction. "I wondered if perhaps marrying a Whig had blinkered you as well."

"Robert may have been a Whig, sir, but he was not a Jacobin. He loathed the revolution as much as you."

"Perhaps he had a redeeming feature after all, then," remarked the Earl smoothly, swirling the cognac again and sniffing it appreciatively. "One thing the French *can* do well is produce an excellent swig— Now, then, where was I? Oh, yes, this shameful peace. I swear, 'Beth, that if you'd been in Town when the news first broke, you'd have thought them all gone completely mad, for there seemed as many revolutionaries in Piccadilly as in every Paris *boulevard* put together. There was no stopping to consider the wicked terms of this treaty, no pause to wonder why England is giving back everything to France, but the French relinquish nothing in return. No, there was no thought of that, there was just the mob, parading through the streets, demanding that every house be illuminated in celebration—and woe betide those who did not hasten to comply! First Consul Bonaparte was their Messiah, and Ambassador Otto's house in Portman Square was become a shrine. I'll warrant the King wondered how long it would be before Madame Guillotine sprang up in Hyde Park."

She smiled as she watched him, for his whole manner smacked of the House of Lords, from the way his head was held back so that his clear, precise voice could carry, to the way he surveyed the invisible ranks of peers somewhere to the rear of Charterleigh's great hall. With a smile, she went to sit on a high-backed settle. "You *have* had a long day in the House, haven't you?" she said.

"I have, indeed, trying to point out the dangers of this iniquitous Treaty of Amiens. Bonaparte is laughing at us, he's successfully swept us to the sidelines, leaving him free to continue annexing Europe to his ever-growing empire. He sees himself as the new Charlemagne, you mark my words! Which brings me to my reason for coming here to-night, 'Beth."

She blinked. "You've come here because Bonaparte aspires to be Holy Roman Emperor? How on earth can that involve me?"

He chuckled. "I admit that the link must appear somewhat tenuous."

"It's not even that, sir, it's completely invisible!"

"It is because of the peace treaty that I've accepted the appointment in Madras, assisting the Governor-General, the Earl of Mornington."

Now she was completely mystified. "But you've always sworn never to take a post abroad—"

"I've sworn many a thing in my time, 'Beth, including never to set foot in this house, but here I am."

"Why have you accepted this post? And what's more to the point, why have you come here?"

"I go to Madras because there are those in the government who, like me, can see Bonaparte for what he is. The terms of the treaty dictate that Britain shall hand back French territories, including those in India—once my province, you will remember."

"I remember."

"It is widely felt that Bonaparte has no intention of meeting any of the terms which are supposed to bind him, and so it has been decided—most secretly, you understand —that there shall be some diplomatic delaying on the side of the British."

"Some fudging, you mean, and who better to do it than you, one of the most expert fudgers in Parliament."

"Do I detect a note of sarcasm?"

"I thought I was praising you," she replied blandly, "for is it not the ambition of every politician to be a notable fudger?

"Hmm. Well, call it what you will, I prefer to call it diplomacy. My skills in the field will be of undoubted assistance to Mornington in his dealings with the French, and I feel it most important that at such a delicate point in our country's history, I should do my utmost to be of assistance."

She was silent for a moment. "I still fail to see what this has to do with me."

"I was coming to that." He looked away from her.

She was immediately suspicious, for his inability to meet another's gaze was his weak point as a politician—and as a card-player. His eyes always wavered when he knew he was on thin ground, and she knew him well enough by now to see that he was in just such a predicament now. "Yes?" she said. "Do go on."

" 'Beth, this was to have been your sister's first Season—"

She stiffened. "No!"

"Please, 'Beth."

"No! Jillian has made her feelings toward me more than

clear, Father, so asking me to oversee her first Season would be an unmitigated disaster.''

"I was hoping that you and she might have made up since that business with Captain Francis.''

"I have been quite amenable and agreeable; Jillian has not.''

"But you were always so close—''

"We no longer are, sir. She still believes I snitched to you about her indiscretions because I was jealous and spiteful. She will not believe that I did it because I was concerned for her, knowing Francis to be a blackguard—I had her best interests at heart, but she is determined not to believe it.''

"She'll come around, 'Beth.''

"She won't, for she believed herself in love with him. Father, it must be obvious to you that I'm not the person to ask. Couldn't Aunt Silchester attend to it?''

"Aunt Silchester was to have done the honors, but she is now too ill to take on the responsibility. There's only you, 'Beth. You're Jillian's elder sister and you're a widow, you're entirely suitable to have charge—''

"You seem to be conveniently forgetting my notorious past, sir. There was a time you believed me to have behaved so shamelessly that you almost disinherited me.''

"But I didn't disinherit you, did I? And besides, you've been an entirely respectable widow for two years now. 'Beth, it is important to me that Jillian be brought out this year, and I need you to do this for me if I am to go to Madras in two days' time without this weight on my shoulders. Please do it, please take charge of your sister's first Season.''

2

Slowly Alabeth got to her feet. "It isn't fair of you to ask me such a thing in such a way, for you place me in an impossible position."

"I have to, for it is imperative that I reach Madras as swiftly as possible. Bonaparte isn't about to sit on his hands while I make my plans in a leisurely way, is he?"

"It may be imperative for you to go to Madras, but it certainly isn't imperative for Jillian to be brought out this year. Why can she not wait until your return?"

"Because I've given her my word." Again his eyes slid away in that uneasy way.

"She's old enough to understand that you have to break your word."

"But I don't *want* to break my word," he cried. "I want her to be launched *this* year. Just think, 'Beth, it's the first Season after eight years of war, and society is determined to make it the most dazzling summer possible."

She held her ground, determined not to give in to the pleading in his eyes. "If I have charge of Jillian, she cannot be guaranteed a dazzling Season, and you know it, Father. To begin with I am still *persona non grata* at Almack's, and a young lady like Jillian would need to be seen there."

"The Duchess of Seaham is prepared to escort your sister to Almack's, for there is no need for you to be caused embarrassment at the hands of those patroness vixens—"

She was aghast. "You've been talking to Octavia about all this?"

"Of course I have, she's your closest friend still, isn't she? Damn it, 'Beth, I'm desperate to get this all sorted out, and Octavia is always guaranteed to be a fount of wisdom."

Alabeth thought of her friend the Duchess, who although fifteen years her senior was most certainly her dearest and most trusted friend. Octavia was cheerful, amusing, and the brightest of London's hostesses. Seaham House rivaled Melbourne House, Devonshire House, and even Carlton House, and invitations there were much sought after by the *ton*. The only blot on the Seaham escutcheon was the noble Duke himself, for he was as dull-witted as his wife was sharp. He had long since deserted the marriage bed in pursuit of a succession of Cyprians, whose intelligence in no way matched the Duchess's and who were only too pleased to be able to boast of having conquered a Duke. Octavia had accepted the situation, finding her spouse decidedly uninspiring anyway, and having discovered that there were many other gentlemen, more charming and witty, with whom she could enjoy liaisons. Yes, Octavia had undoubtedly sinned a great deal more than Alabeth had ever done, but she was accepted at Almack's and Alabeth was not, having committed the unforgivable sin of being at the center of a *cause célèbre*, having flouted convention, and having stepped on the sensitive toes of the Treguard family, whose tentacles reached throughout society, even in the Royal Family itself.

The Earl cleared his throat. "Octavia said I was to do my utmost to persuade you to take Jillian on. She said that you'd be the best person to do it and that anyway you'd enjoy Town again if only you'd give it a chance."

"Octavia has never stopped trying to persuade me."

"She's right."

"I'm not ready to take society on again yet, Father."

"Nonsense, you're wilting away out here in rural seclusion. What you need is the diversion of London's drawing rooms.''

"I'm perfectly happy here, and am determined to remain here, dazzling Season or no dazzling Season.''

He searched in his pockets then and drew out some papers and cards. "Look at all these, 'Beth, and see then if you feel so strongly. You may have offended the Treguards in the past, but it's over now, especially as Robert is no longer with us. There is even an invitation to Carlton House, surely proof enough that you are welcome back into the fold.''

Reluctantly she took them. Without exception they were invitations to events of the highest class, including, as he said, a fete at Carlton House, where the Prince of Wales' guests of honor would be luminaries from the French world of art, this being the Prince's contribution to the new peace. She set the gold-edged card aside and looked at the next, an invitation to a grand regatta at Ranelagh Gardens, to be followed by a feast in the Rotunda and a magnificent firework display. The other cards announced masquerades, routs, assemblies, dinner parties, supper parties, boating parties, and even breakfast parties. There were to be numerous balls—including, of course, Octavia Seaham's famous annual ball on the King's birthday—and there was a special dispensation for ladies to visit the British Museum. There was the private viewing at the Royal Academy, Ascot week, the opera season— The list was endless, and as exciting to her as her father knew it would be, for he was right when he said she needed the diversions of London, for she was born to revel in a high society life.

The Earl saw indecision creep into her eyes, and he pressed home his advantage. "You'd have the full use of the house in Berkeley Square, and ample funds to cover any eventuality—including the most lavish of balls for Jillian.''

She hesitated on the brink of agreement, and then drew back. "No, I cannot do it."

"But why? Is it because you fear encountering Castleton?"

"Sir Piers Castleton has not entered my thoughts," she replied stiffly.

"It is immaterial, anyway, for the fellow is about to take himself off to Europe, touring all those places which have been closed to us because of the war."

"I don't refuse because of him."

"Why, then?"

"Because I know that Jillian will not come around to it, she simply will *not* consent to be put in my charge."

"Ah, but I believe she will, for there is a very enticing lure."

"What lure?"

"A certain Polish aristocrat by the name of Count Adam Zaleski."

"Who?"

"Oh, come now, surely you're heard of him—the darling of the First Consul, the matchless poet of the pianoforte. Surely a newspaper reaches this outlandish spot from time to time?"

She smiled. "Now you mention it, I have heard of him."

"Well, the signing of the peace treaty has resulted in him deciding to honor London with his presence, giving recitals and so on. He is also intending to give tuition to certain favored pupils. Your sister wishes to be one of that select band; she wishes it so much that I believe she will agree to be in your charge."

"She *must* admire this Zaleski person," remarked Alabeth dryly.

"She does, and rightly so, for he is acknowledged to be the greatest exponent of the pianoforte in the world, and I am told he justly deserves his reputation. 'Beth, that business with Captain Francis is over now and should be forgotten. I believe I can guarantee Jillian's agreement—and so all I need is yours. Please, 'Beth, do what I beg of you.''

Something in his tone warned her that he was still uneasy, and sure enough, when she looked at him, he could not meet her gaze. ''Father, is there anything you're not telling me?''

''Not telling you? Why ever do you ask that?''

''Because I know you very well.''

''There isn't anything.'' He met her gaze then, but she knew he was finding it difficult. There *was* something else, but he was determined not to divulge it, and she could hardly pursue the point without virtually accusing him of lying.

Outside, another rumble of thunder wandered across the heavens, closer now, for the flash of lightning which followed came almost simultaneously, glinting on the suits of armor standing around the great hall.

''Will you do it, 'Beth?''

Reluctantly she nodded. ''Very well.''

He looked relieved. ''Thank you, my dear. I don't think you'll ever know how grateful I am to you.'' He turned to pick up his hat and gloves from a nearby table. ''And now, I must return to Town—''

''You aren't staying the night?''

''I've very little time to set all my affairs in order. I'll see that the Berkeley Square house is in readiness and that my solicitors are aware of what plans have been made. By the way . . .''

''Yes?''

''Don't let's beat about the bush, for we both know that the whole purpose of bringing a young lady out is to find a suitable husband for her. I believe that your own experience will make you an excellent judge of who is and who is not suitable for your sister.''

''Meaning?''

"Meaning that, unfortunately, we all learn from our mistakes."

Her chin came up at that. "My marriage to Robert was not a mistake."

"Forgive me, my dear, but I believe it was. The fact that by some miracle you and Robert were happy together does not make one iota of difference. He was everything that was unsuitable. Maybe you managed because your character is different, a little stronger, but Jillian would be entirely unable to cope with a gentlemen like Robert, and I believe you know it. She is impressionable and impetuous, given entirely to romantic daydreamings, and she would be at the mercy of a charming rogue like Manvers. Forgive me, my dear, for I don't wish to sound hard or thoughtless, for I know how much he meant to you, but I beg you to understand how I fear those like him when I consider how Jillian will react to them. The gentlemen she will encounter this coming Season will fall into two categories—they will be either suitable or unsuitable. Those like Sir Charles Allister, the son of my dearest friend, are entirely suitable, for there is nothing I would like more than to see him allied with Jillian. Those like Sir Piers Castleton, who is in some ways as notorious as Robert was, for he too has been involved in unsavory duels, are most definitely *un*suitable."

She smiled a little. "But unfortunately it is the likes of Piers Castleton who have the charm and engaging manners."

"I believe it was ever thus," he agreed, sighing heavily at the injustices of life.

"You may rely on me to do everything as you would wish it and to always have Jillian's best interests at heart."

He kissed her fondly on the cheek. "Forgive me for my past stubbornness, my dear, but you were a very precious kitten to me."

She stood beneath the stone porch watching his carriage

drive away through the storm. Thunder ranged over the dark skies again and the wind soughed through the trees of the park, tearing blossoms from the nearby cherry orchards. She could hear the crash of the English Channel on the shore some distance away, and the lanterns swung so wildly on their chains that they cast eerie shadows over the fierce stone griffins guarding the entrance to the house. She was filled with misgivings about the wisdom of her decision, and filled with an uneasy suspicion that there was something her father had not told her—the real cause of his determination to bring Jillian out that year and no other.

The carriage vanished from sight beyond the windblown rhododendrons, and holding her shawl closely around her shoulders, she went back into the house, her steps taking her inevitably up to the long gallery where Robert's portrait held pride of place. Lighting a candle from one of the wall brackets, she approached the great door of the gallery, and it creaked loudly as she opened it.

The portrait seemed to spring to life in the candlelight, and his lazy blue eyes laughed at her again. For a breathless moment she even imagined she heard his low, teasing voice, but there was only the silence of the house and the raging of the storm outside. The candle flickered over his face. How handsome he had been with his graceful figure and curly fair hair, he was at once effortlessly elegant and nonchalantly casual, and it was typical of him that his irrepressible humor should come through even in such a formal portrait.

Tears shone in her green eyes as she traced the outline of his lips with her fingertip. How enchanted their first meeting had been. He had made her cast caution to the winds, made her want to flout convention, do anything just to be with him. It had not mattered that he was said to be such a wicked rakehell; she knew only that he was loving and gentle, witty and charming, that his eyes could court her with a glance and his kiss melt her very soul.

These two years without him had been the longest of her life. Each morning she had awakened alone, reaching instinctively to touch him, but the warm memories had fled when her searching fingers had found the bed cold and empty— But he would have been with her still had it not been for that needless, senseless duel, a duel which could so easily have been avoided had it not been for the presence of Sir Piers Castleton.

For a moment her emotions threatened to overwhelm her and she turned sharply away from the portrait, the shadows leaping all around as the candle guttered. She felt as if Piers' mocking gray eyes were watching her from somewhere beyond the edge of the light, and the anger which only he could arouse stirred darkly in her heart until she halted suddenly, lowering her gaze to the swaying flame. This would not do, for what point was there in it? Robert was gone forever, and reminding herself of Piers Castleton's guilt would not bring him back again. It was 1802 now and tonight she had accepted a responsibility which would sweep her back into the gaiety of London society, back into that life which she had once loved so much. She must try to forget the past and begin again.

Determined not to look back at the portrait, she walked along the gallery, but as she reached the doorway, she could not help turning, just to take one last, lingering look. She could not stem the yearning which ached through her still. He had gone, and it was Piers Castleton who was to blame.

3

A week later than planned, Alabeth at last set off for London, her maroon traveling carriage taking the narrow coast road through Oakingham to the main London-to-Dover highway. She chose this route, which was not the most direct, because she loved the wild scenery and knew it would be some time before she saw it again. Inland, the Kent countryside was undulating, a region of hop-growing and cherry orchards, but here on the coast itself there were tidal creeks with low islands where there were thousands of seabirds, and there were miles of flat green marsh inhabited only by sheep and cattle. It was perhaps a rather desolate landscape, but to her it was very special indeed, for it was part of her life with Robert. How many times had she ridden or driven along this quiet track with him? Too many to remember, perhaps, and yet remember them she did, for each one was so precious . . .

The team's hooves clattered pleasantly on the dusty road as she gazed out at the mouth of the Thames estuary where the water glittered and sparkled in the early May sun. A Royal Navy frigate was beating seaward, her sails very white against the jade-green waves and her gunports closed now after being eight years in readiness.

Alabeth's gloved hands were clasped neatly in her lap and her reticule rested on the velvet seat beside her. She wore a brown hat adorned with golden tassels, a neat spencer of the same brown, and a white spotted muslin gown, its hem trimmed with several rows of chestnut satin ribbon. She gazed out the window, her feelings mixed. She had tried to convince herself that returning to London society would be a sovereign remedy after the despondency of the past two years, but now that the moment was upon her, she was once again filled with trepidation.

She had received a hurried note from her father, informing her that Jillian had come around to the whole idea, but there had been no communication from Jillian herself, no olive branch to offer some hope that the coming months would be pleasant and carefree. Reading between the lines of the Earl's letter, Alabeth had guessed that Jillian had not been easy to convince, in spite of the imminent presence in Town of Count Adam Zaleski, and now Alabeth found herself wishing more and more that she had refused to have anything to do with her sister's first Season. With a sigh she stared out the window. The tide was beginning to come in over the saltings, the water gleaming among the reeds and mud flats. In summer this place would be bright with golden samphire, but she would not see it; she would be enduring months in London which she feared were going to be odious in the extreme, and not the new beginning she had so vainly hoped they would be.

The carriage neared Oakingham with its ancient medieval gateway. In times gone by, the town had been a thriving port, but now it stood several hundred yards from the sea because the marsh had filled the natural harbor, leaving only the winding channel of the River Keble to link the once-busy quay with the open water. Only small fishing boats could negotiate the river, but in nearby creeks were to be found the swift smuggling vessels which made Oakingham so notorious still. The former Prime Minister, Mr. Pitt, and his government had done much to stamp out the trade in contraband, but here in Oakingham it flourished, its citizens as determined to defy the law as the revenue men were determined to enforce it. But today, with the sun shining brightly over the blossoms in the orchards and the flowers in the gardens behind the weatherboarded houses, it was hard to imagine the little town as anything but law-abiding.

Wheels rattling and harness jingling, the carriage passed beneath the stone gateway and began the climb up the narrow street, passing tidy shops and inns, crossing a quiet, leafy square overlooked by the church, and then soon leaving the little town behind as the road turned inland to join the busy highway linking the capital with the important channel port of Dover.

On the main road the coach came up to a smarter pace, the team stepping high as they trotted along. A mail coach flew by, posthorn blaring and dust flying as it strove to keep to its strict schedule. Alabeth settled back. She was well on her way now and there was no turning back.

The carriage had not proceeded very much farther when suddenly it swerved violently and she heard the coachman shouting angrily. The team whinnied and she had to clutch at the seat to save herself from falling as the carriage lurched to a sudden standstill, the coachman shouting again and this time being answered by another, equally angry, voice from a little farther along the road.

Alabeth lowered the glass to see what had happened. Ahead there was another carriage, a very elegant drag lacquered in olive-green and drawn by the most perfectly matched grays she had ever seen, and from its position she could see that it had been about to overtake a carrier's wagon and that her own coachman had obviously mis-judged its distance and speed and had almost collided with it. She glanced at the crest on the olive-green door, but even as a gasp of dismayed recognition escaped her lips, the door opened and a gentleman alighted, pausing in the road to toy with his frilled cuffs as he glanced up with some annoyance at his gesticulating coachman, who was brandishing his fist and hurling obscenities at Alabeth's coachman. Alabeth heard nothing, saw nothing, except that the gentleman was only too well known to her, and that his name was Sir Piers Castleton.

His tall hat was tipped back on his head and he wore a charcoal-gray coat which fitted his excellent figure to perfection, its high stand-fall collar emphasizing the broadness of his shoulders. His Florentine waistcoat was pale blue and his beige breeches clung revealingly to his slender hips. A sapphire pin shone in the folds of his neckcloth, spurs glittered on his top boots, and all in all he looked very much a gentleman of rank and fashion. He had changed little since last she had seen him, except perhaps that he was a little more bronzed, and was still darkly handsome with his tangle of almost-black curls and his clear, penetrating gray eyes. His eyes always caught the attention the most, for there was a light in them which warned that he was not a man to be trifled with—as a certain unfortunate Russian diplomat had once found out. The Russian's death in the ensuing duel had caused uproar in government circles; the Czar had been most put out at the death of one of his favorites, and Piers had been forced to quit the country for a time until the awkwardness could be smoothed over, for Piers was as much a favorite with the Prince of Wales as the Russian had been with the Czar. Would to God it had never been smoothed over, she thought, watching him, for then he would never have come back to England, never have entered Robert's life, and never have destroyed her world.

She felt quite numb with the shock of seeing him, for she had believed him far away in Europe somewhere, but then, as if he sensed the close scrutiny, he turned suddenly to look straight at her, recognizing her immediately even though she drew sharply back. She was thrown into total confusion, her poise completely shaken, but she struggled to be mistress of herself and presented a collected appearance when at last she heard his steps approaching and the door was thrown open.

"Lady Alabeth." He inclined his head. His voice was just as she remembered, softly spoken but firm, and always with that hint of mockery she loathed so much.

"Sir."

"Am I to glean from your cool manner that your attitude has not mellowed these past two years?"

"You are."

"Dear me, how tiresome, for I understand that you are honoring society with your presence again this year."

"I am."

"Then I trust that either our paths do not cross again or that you are able to mend your manners sufficiently to behave with some decorum when next they do."

Her cheeks flamed. "How dare you speak to me like that!"

"I daresay the talent to be rude comes as easily to me as it does to you," he replied, his glance wandering over her. "You are as lovely as ever, madam. It is a pity that your character does not match your appearance."

"And you are as vile as ever, sir," she breathed, quivering with anger, "deserving nothing but my contempt."

His smile was cool, a light passing through his gray eyes. "Indeed? How very determined you are to hate me, almost too determined, I fancy."

"I loathe you sufficiently to tell you that had I known you would be in England after all, I would not have undertaken to come to Town."

"You have the perfidious French to thank for my change of plans, for it is obvious to me that they mean this peace to be temporary, and I have no wish to be trapped in some far place when Bonaparte makes his next empire-building move. I shall of a certainty be in Town over the coming months, madam, and if the fact bothers you to that extent, perhaps you should order your coachman to turn back to Charterleigh immediately—that is, if the dolt can manage such a complicated basic maneuver."

She flushed at the implication that her man was completely at fault. "I believe your own fellow needs a lesson or two, sir, for it is but a simple matter to glance behind and see if anyone else has had the temerity to use the King's high road. As to my returning to Charterleigh, let me tell you that nothing would make me change my plans to suit you, sir."

"A change of your attitude would suit me, madam. Your plans matter not one jot."

"My attitude toward you will *never* change!"

"Then I can only believe that you glory in your misguidedness," he replied, closing the door on her and turning to walk back to his own carriage.

She was so angry that she could hardly speak, gesturing to her coachman to proceed and then drawing up the glass with a snap. She kept her eyes averted as she passed Piers, but she was aware of the derisive way he doffed his hat.

She knew that she had handled the unexpected meeting very badly; she had allowed her emotions to interfere with etiquette and had thus failed abysmally to get the better of him. She had never been able to get the better of him, she reflected, for he always so thoroughly ruffled her feathers that her poise crumbled into nothing, leaving her feeling gauche and uneasy.

Suddenly the prospect of London seemed more awful than ever, for not only would she have to contend with Jillian's resentment, she would know that every time she left the house, every function she attended, every drive she took, she ran the certain risk of encountering Sir Piers Castleton. She had told her father that Piers had not crossed her mind, but that was not true, for he had crossed her mind a great deal, because she could not forget him or ignore his existence.

Piers stood in the roadway, watching her carriage drive away. How very lovely she was, as lovely as a rose, and covered with as many damned thorns! She was obviously quite set upon blaming him for Robert's fall from grace, and that was tedious enough, but to be faced with the certainty of those thorns throughout the coming Season was intolerable. Piers Castleton was not a man to endure the disagreeable for very long, and Alabeth was obviously determined to be as disagreeable as possible. Well, she would regret it if she persisted, he thought, tugging his hat forward on his unruly hair and climbing back into his carriage. He lounged back on the seat, a pensive smile touching his lips as he thought of the haughty redheaded lady in the maroon traveling carriage. He would give her a little time, but if she showed no signs of changing her tune, then perhaps he would have to forget he was a gentleman, and point out to the lady the error of her ways!

4

It was dusk when Alabeth's carriage turned into Berkeley Square, threading past the crowd of carriages outside Gunter's, where the *beau monde* was sampling the famous ices and confectionery. The square was not square at all, its east and west sides being much longer than the others, and it sloped away, its center filled with young plane trees. She gazed out at the trees as they rustled their spring foliage in the slight breeze. She could remember them being planted thirteen years before, when she had been only ten; before then it had been very bare.

Outside each exclusive house there was a footman parading importantly up and down, waiting for guests to call, and outside her father's house there was also such a footman, very splendid in Wallborough gray and cream, and he hurried forward immediately as the carriage came to a standstill. He opened the door and lowered the steps, and she alighted, pausing for a while on the pavement. The perfume of the plane trees filled the air and she heard some laughter from Gunter's. She felt tired, not because the journey from Charterleigh had been long, but because it had been broken by that trying confrontation with Piers Castleton and because it would be ended with another, similar confrontation, this time with Jillian. She looked up at the house's elegant facade, its windows bright with lights and its front door approached by a flight of shallow steps passing beneath a wrought-iron arch from which was suspended a particularly beautiful lamp. Taking a deep breath, she went up the steps, the door opening magically before her as Sanderson, the butler, anticipated the moment exactly.

The tiled vestibule was a cool green, lighted by an immense chandelier and made bright by a large bowl of spring flowers, brought fresh from Covent Garden market that morning. A long-case clock ticked steadily in the recess next to the Adam fireplace, and from the music room several floors above echoed the soft notes of the pianoforte—Jillian was playing Scarlatti.

Alabeth turned to the butler. "Good evening, Sanderson."

"Good evening, my lady. Welcome home."

She smiled. "Is everything in order?"

"Yes, my lady."

"Did my father leave any further instructions for me?"

"No, my lady, but there are a number of cards and invitations." He brought a large silver salver from a table.

She glanced quickly through them, wondering how on earth anyone could be expected to attend all of the functions which society seemed set upon this Season, for, to be sure, one would need the constitution of an ox. Among the cards, she noticed that Sir Charles Allister had already called. "When did Sir Charles call?" she asked.

"This afternoon, my lady, but there was no one at home. Lady Jillian had gone to call upon Lady Silchester."

"And how is my aunt?"

"As well as can be expected, my lady, but I gather from Lady Jillian that she is certainly well enough to find fault with everything." The butler cleared his throat and sniffed a little; he and Lady Silchester had never seen eye to eye, and he was of sufficient importance in the house to hint as much, having been with the Earl of Wallborough since the Earl's seafaring days in the Royal Navy.

Alabeth smiled. "Then I imagine that my aunt is well on

the road to recovery," she remarked, removing the pins from her hat and handing it to him.

"Indeed so, my lady."

"I take it that that is my sister playing the pianoforte?"

"It is, my lady."

"Then I will go to her."

"Shall you require any refreshment, my lady?"

"A little cold supper, perhaps—and a glass of my favorite wine."

"I have a bottle on ice, my lady."

She mounted the black marble staircase which ascended from the far end of the vestibule, her gloved hand sliding easily on the polished mahogany rail and her shadow moving across the wall beside her. The crystal drops of the chandelier flashed and the light fell pleasingly over her father's prized collection of paintings by Canaletto. Tall Ionic columns guarded the head of the staircase, stretching up into the darkness high above, and the music was louder now, the rippling notes played with an exquisite touch.

She reached the second floor and walked along the passage, passing the camphorwood chests with their strange oriental perfume, and then at last she was at the door of the music room. Inside she could see her sister seated at the Broadwood pianoforte, her head bowed as she played.

Lady Jillian Carstairs was very beautiful, and her golden hair, a startling contrast to Alabeth's dark red, was cut in the short style known as the Titus, a boyish fashion which emphasized the daintiness of her face. She wore a lilac lawn gown, its low neckline made modest and becoming by the insertion of a white tucker with three dainty frills at the throat. There was a golden locket resting on the tucker and a small fob watch pinned beneath the gown's very high waistline. She looked quite exquisite, but there was a set to her mouth which told immediately that she was well aware of her sister's presence in the doorway, although the music did not falter and she did not glance up for even a second.

At last the final notes died away and she removed her hands from the keys. "Good evening, Alabeth." The tone was not welcoming.

"Good evening, Jillian. I congratulate you upon your playing, I have seldom heard better."

"I don't want your congratulations."

"Jillian . . ."

"I don't want to have to put up with you at all."

"That's quite enough."

"Is it?" Jillian stood, her blue eyes flashing with a bitter anger. "I don't think it's anywhere near enough. Why should I have to do your bidding? Why should I be obedient toward you, when in your time you obeyed no one?"

"Did you give your word to Father that you would accept this situation?"

Jillian looked away, her lips pressed stubbornly together.

"Well, did you?" pressed Alabeth.

"And if I did?"

"Then you must stand by that word . . . as I am doing."

"I'll warrant it pleases you immensely to be able to order me about."

"I promise you that it doesn't please me at all and that as I look at you right now, I wish with all my heart that I had refused to have anything to do with this idiotic notion of Father's—but I agreed and so help me I will do my best. Jillian, I don't want to continue quarreling with you, for you are my sister and until now we have always got on so well together—"

"That was before you told tales about me to Father last summer."

"They weren't 'tales,' and anyway, you left me no choice."

"You didn't have to tell him anything."

"Jillian, you were being very indiscreet, and with a man who could hardly claim to be a gentleman."

"I loved him, and you ruined my chances of happiness with him."

"He omitted to tell you he had a wife."

"Even if he had been single, your actions would have been the same. Your only motive was a jealous spite, a determination to deny me the sort of happiness you had known with Robert. You eloped with one of the most notorious men in England, but you had the gall to tell Father that I had taken a stroll with Captain Francis. It was a despicable act, Alabeth, and I shall never forgive you."

"I had to tell him, because I could see only too well what the good Captain's intentions were. You were on the road to ruin, Jillian, and I cared enough for you to do my utmost to put a stop to it."

"Oh, and you succeeded," cried Jillian, quivering with fury.

"Then you may thank your lucky stars," said Alabeth, remaining commendably calm in the face of such unjust accusations, "for you came through it all unscathed, your reputation intact."

"Which can hardly be said of you," replied Jillian, her glance and tone calculated to be as insolent and provocative as possible.

Alabeth took a deep breath. "At least Robert intended to marry me. Oh, Jillian, why are you like this? I admit that I was disobedient, that I caused a scandal, but perhaps it is *because* I did those things that I know what I'm talking about. The pitfalls are there, they trapped me, and so I can see them now—and I can warn you, see that you don't stumble into them."

"You just want to deny me the sort of love and happiness you had. You're a dog-in-the-manger, Alabeth, and I hate you."

Alabeth stared at her. "You don't really mean that," she said incredulously, "for I simply will not believe it."

"I don't care what you believe. In fact, I don't care anything about you." Jillian's chin was raised defiantly, her whole attitude challenging.

"Very well," said Alabeth, "then I shall use the powers at my disposal."

"What powers?"

"The powers given to me by Father when he asked me to take on this responsibility. *In loco parentis,* I believe the phrase is. Now, then, are you going to undertake to be agreeable?"

"No."

"Very well, you must go to your room."

Jillian stared at her. "Go to my room?"

"I am not about to put up with your present behavior—of that you may be certain—and until I see some significant improvement, I shall refuse to begin your Season."

"But you can't—"

"Oh, yes, I can. I am not prepared to launch you upon society when I cannot be sure if you will behave yourself. Can you imagine my taking you to Carlton House, fearing all the time that you might make a scene? Oh, no, Jillian Carstairs, I am not that much of a fool and so shall not stick my neck out at all to suit you. Nor will I be obliging in any way, so you may certainly forget any notion you have of receiving tuition from Count Adam Zaleski."

"You cannot mean that!" Jillian gasped, obviously horrified to realize the full extent of Alabeth's control over her.

"I mean every word, Jillian—unless, of course, you are prepared to stand by your promise to Father."

Jillian turned away, biting her lip. Until this moment she had believed that she could continue with the feud, speak as she pleased and behave as she saw fit; now it seemed that such conduct would punish not Alabeth, but herself.

Alabeth hated being so authoritarian, for it was not in her character, but she knew that unless she took a stand now, the situation would become intolerable. Jillian was like a stranger, so very different from the sweet, vivacious girl she had known before the advent of Captain Francis the previous year. Until he had arrived in Wallborough Castle they had always been so close, sharing laughter and secrets, but not any more. Jillian was now cold and distant, seeming really to hate her. And all because of a man who did not merit even a second thought . . .

Jillian turned back toward her at last. "Very well," she said in a low voice, "I have no choice but to agree, but I will only do as I have to, and no more."

"That will do to be going on with, for I will put up with what I have to, and no more." Alabeth walked from the room, pausing in the doorway to look back. "Jillian, I truly don't wish to go on in this vein, for I love you very much.

Jillian looked at her without saying a word, and at last Alabeth walked on out. She was shaking as she descended the staircase, for the meeting had been worse than she had imagined. In fact, everything was worse than she had imagined, for she must also endure Piers Castleton's presence in Town. Oh, how she wished she was back in the seclusion of Charterleigh!

5

The following morning Jillian decided very pointedly to take her breakfast in her room, thus avoiding facing Alabeth across the table. Alabeth did not know whether to be relieved or dismayed, for while it spared her the immediate prospect of another unpleasant meeting, it also prolonged the agony, for they must meet again sooner or later. She sat alone in the sun-drenched morning room, toying with her coffee and staring at the butter nestling in its dish of ice. Outside, the tiny rear garden was filled with spring color, from the daffodils and tulips in the beds to the almond blossom and forsythia above, but it was robbed of any true atmosphere because it was walled in, reminding her forcibly that this was the heart of Mayfair, not the heart of Kent.

"My lady?" Sanderson appeared at her elbow.

"Yes?"

"The Duchess of Seaham has called."

Alabeth was taken aback, for nobody called before eleven o'clock in the morning. "Very well, show her in."

A moment later Octavia bustled brightly into the room in a flurry of orange and white taffeta, her bonnet ribbons streaming and her rouged face beaming as she bent to kiss Alabeth on the cheek. "My *dearest* Alabeth, how glad I am to see you, for I swear I feared to this very moment that you would turn and scuttle back to your lair."

Alabeth smiled. "How are you, Octavia?"

"Well, as you see." The Duchess sat in the chair Sanderson drew out for her, but shook her head when he offered her coffee.

"So," said Alabeth, "you haven't joined the throngs hastening over to Paris?"

"My dear, I wouldn't trust the French farther than I could throw them; they are all assassins, every last one of them, with Bonaparte the assassin-in-chief."

"I thought at the very least you'd have toddled off to see the latest in fashions."

"I don't need to see them, I've heard enough. I'm told that Parisiennes wear a gauze so shockingly transparent that there is nothing a gentleman cannot see. Where's the allure in that? Where's the mystery? Why bother with seduction when the world has already ravished with its leering eyes?" Octavia sniffed. "No breeding, that's their trouble."

"Oh, naturally," murmured Alabeth roguishly.

Octavia cast a baleful glance at her. "That's quite enough of that from you, missy, especially as you've only just condescended to rejoin the human race."

"I was quite enjoying life at Charterleigh."

"Nonsense, how can anyone enjoy a dull existence out in the wilds of Kent! I'll set you straight again now. You mark my words, I'll have you married off before the Season is out."

"I don't want to be married off."

"What rubbish. Of course you do. Why else agree to come to Town?"

"Octavia, your matchmaking activities are too much at times. I've come to Town to bring Jillian out, and that is my only reason."

"Oh, how dull of you. I was so hoping to be able to matchmake for you both, now I'll have to content myself with just Jillian."

"She's handful enough, even for you," remarked Alabeth with feeling.

Octavia sat back. "I gather she's troublesome."

"She's resentful."

"Foolish chit."

"Well, she believes she's justified."

"So your father told me. I'm of the opinion that she should be put over someone's knee and given a good spanking."

"Well, she's promised to be agreeable."

"How very noble of her. She should be grateful you've agreed to do her this considerable service."

"She certainly isn't grateful."

"She's a spoiled little minx, and I told your father as much."

Alabeth laughed. "And what did he say to that?"

"What could he say? He was forced to agree, because the evidence is there for all to see."

Alabeth's smile faded. "Octavia, I don't suppose . . ."

"Yes?"

"Well, he didn't say anything else to you, did he? Something about why he was so very determined to bring Jillian out this year?"

"No, but now you come to mention it, he did seem a little too anxious about it."

"That's what I thought. There's something I haven't been told and should have been."

"Oh, surely not. After all, if it was anything important, he would cerrtainly have informed you, for it wouldn't be right not to."

"I hope you're right."

"Of course I am, and you're not to go worrying about it. Now, then, we have things to discuss."

"Things?"

"If I'm to obtain a voucher from Almack's for Jillian."

"Oh, yes."

"I take it that you will not be honoring that dull place with your presence."

"Too many of the lady patronesses are friendly with too

many Treguards and I'm not about to offer myself for execution at the hands of those hypocritical *chiennes*."

Octavia chuckled. "I can't entirely blame you, and I swear that Almack's is the end in *ennui,* but unfortunately it is *de rigueur* to be seen there for someone like Jillian. I am quite prepared to take her on, and woe betide her if she steps out of line with me."

"She won't, she's an angel with everyone except me."

"Good, then I shall proceed with the arrangements. And talking about arrangements, what have you decided to do about Jillian's ball?"

"I haven't decided anything yet."

"I trust that you intend to call upon me for advice."

"As if I would do anything else!"

"There's nothing more I adore than organizing a grand ball, and I'd simply never forgive you if you left me out." Then, as if it was all a foregone conclusion, she proceeded, "I thought we'd hold it at Seaham House, which after all boasts one of the most exquisite ballrooms in Town."

"That's very kind of you, Octavia."

"Nonsense, it's very selfish of me, for that way I'm certain to be in the thick of it." Octavia smiled. "I trust that you and Jillian are coming to my little affair on the King's birthday?"

"Little affair?" Alabeth laughed. "Since when has your grand ball been a little affair? It's a national institution from which it's a positive disgrace to be excluded. And, yes, we are definitely accepting the invitation."

"Good, because I've made the coup of the Season," beamed Octavia, exuding triumph. "I've even beaten Carlton House to it."

"To what?"

"Why, Count Adam Zaleski, of course."

"The gentleman who plays the pianoforte?"

"That is to understate his brilliance, for I'm told that

he's a joy, a wizard, a positive genius—added to which he's said to be the most handsome creature imaginable. And he's playing first at my ball.''

"That is indeed a coup."

"I'm very pleased with myself, for it required some very subtle skulduggery on my part, to say nothing of bribing his valet to put my communication before his master first.''

"You don't change, do you?"

"I sincerely hope not."

"You are fortunate that Seaham can afford your extravagances.''

Octavia sniffed. "Seaham has little choice in the matter, for if he kicked up about it, I'd make no end of noise about his Cyprians.''

"That's blackmail."

"He deserves it, for he forsook the marriage bed within months of the wedding. Not that I minded, for, to be sure, he is a clumsy fellow—as his Cyprians would tell him if they didn't admire his purse so greatly. Actually, I wrong his latest amour by calling her a Cyprian, for although she is indeed an impure, she is an aristocratic one.''

"Who is she?"

"Lady Adelina Carver."

"The Earl of Canby's daughter?"

Octavia sniffed again. "The morals of a she-cat, just like her mother. Well, an actress as Countess of Canby, what else can one expect of the offspring of such a union? She's flitted from lover to lover like a bee seeking honey, and the latest noble name on the list happens to be Seaham's. Not that he'd stand a chance with her if the one she really wants would come up trumps. She's only interested in Harry Ponsonby, you know, and has been for over a year now, but although he visits her frequently, she can't get him to the altar.''

"And so Seaham's guilty conscience supports your extravagant entertaining?''

"It does indeed, and serve him right. Although, I must confess that recently I may have gone a little far, even for me."

"In what way?"

"Well, I have arranged a boating party on the lake at Stoneleigh Park, and one simply cannot go to anyone else but Gunter's for the luncheon hampers, but my *dear,* they are two hundred guineas each this year. I've ordered one hundred and fifty, naturally, but I don't think Seaham will be very amused, especially when there is also the cost of the champagne, transporting the golden barge, decorating the island for the feast, hiring the orchestra—to say nothing of the costumes and so on for Charles Allister's masque—"

Alabeth could almost sympathize with the Duke. "Oh, Octavia . . ."

"I know, but really, if one is going to do something, one must do it well, mustn't one?"

"It seems one must."

"And when dear Charles told me about his masque, I simply had to include it."

"What is it, an improving tract for spendthrift wives?"

"Hardly, my dear, for Charles Allister has more money than sense, and he is extravagant by nature."

"And how is he?"

"Flourishing, but still too nice for the wretches of London society, and that's a fact. Truly, he's a catch for some enterprising wench, for he's a darling." Octavia paused. "I agree with your dear Father, Charles Allister is perfect for Jillian."

"I don't know that I'd wish Jillian, in her present mood, on Old Nick himself, let alone poor Charles."

"Hmm, well, she'll come around in the end, you see if she doesn't. Anyway, I simply must go, for I've a hundred and one things to do before luncheon."

"Are you starting a new fashion for calling at breakfast time?"

"There aren't enough hours in the day, Alabeth, so I'm simply being sensible. Oh, by the way, you and Jillian simply must come to the British Museum. I've managed to get a special dispensation for the party to include ladies— for, as you know, we are normally excluded—but provided the party is fifteen in total, then we ladies are included. Is that not excellent? You will come, won't you?"

"I can't say the idea bowls me over."

"My dear, the only reason I wish to go is so that I can look superior and remark that I cannot imagine why gentlemen seek to exclude us from such dull places. They are so insufferable, Alabeth, treating us as if we are inferior, and I simply cannot resist poking their snouts for them at every opportunity."

Alabeth smiled. "Oh, if that's the case, then I shall definitely come and assist you in your heinous activities."

"That's better, I was beginning to despair of you." Octavia got up, but then her smiled faded. "I *am* glad you've come back into the fold, Alabeth, for it wasn't right for you to immure yourself in Charterleigh like that."

"It wasn't like that."

"No?" Octavia's brown eyes were shrewd. "Tell me honestly, would you have undone a single thing had you your time all over again?"

Alabeth looked at her in surprise. "No. Why?"

"Oh, it's just that— Well, I did wonder if—" She smiled in embarrassment. "Oh, it doesn't matter."

"Please tell me."

"I just wondered if you were quite as happy as you made out—I mean, Robert seemed the perfect husband for a long time, but he was returning to his bad old ways, wasn't he? He was spending more and more time at gaming hells, and he came very close to another duel before the one in which he died."

Alabeth looked away. "It wasn't his fault, Octavia, the fault was Sir Piers Castleton's."

"Oh." Octavia straightened. "You do know that Piers is in Town, don't you?"

"Yes."

"He's on everyone's list, my own included. You're bound to see him."

"I know."

"I shall be very honest with you, my dear," Octavia said gently, "I thought you had made a dreadful mistake when you married Robert, for although he was so handsome and charming, there was something in his character, a flaw which would have emerged sooner or later whether Piers Castleton had been there or not. Robert earned his reputation as a rakehell, Alabeth, and he did so without any help from anyone."

"He was reformed," replied Alabeth staunchly. "He had changed his ways and would have remained like that had it not been for Piers."

"A leopard don't change his spots, my dear."

"Are you defending Piers?"

"No, I'm not defending anyone, except perhaps you, although you can't see it. Piers is no angel and I've never pretended that he was."

"He provoked that duel with the Russian."

"I don't deny it, but I think you'll find that there was a lot more to that duel than met the eye, certainly more than the paltry disagreement over cards which brought Robert so determinedly to his death."

Alabeth stared at her. "Why have you never spoken like this before?"

"Because since Robert's death you have remained at Charterleigh and I have seen you only there, wearing black and grieving for him as if there would never be an end to the heartbreak. I could not speak ill of him, not under those circumstances."

"And now?"

"Now I feel I must speak out, for I cannot hold my

tongue anymore. He wasn't right for you, my dear, as you would have found out quite miserably, had he not died when he did. Robert was the perfect lover, Alabeth, but he was no husband; his cloth was cut all wrong for that." Octavia smiled gently. "Am I in dreadful hot water with you now?"

Alabeth could not help returning the smile, for it was impossible to be really angry with Octavia. "You know that you are not."

Octavia kissed her on the cheeks again, enveloping her in a cloud of Yardley's lavender water. "I am so relieved to hear you say that."

"And to prove it I will tell you that you are still invited to my first dinner party next week and that I shall still suffer you sitting next to me."

Octavia grinned. "That, my dear, was a bucket of *cold* water." Her taffeta skirts rustled as she went to the door, which Sanderson hurried to open for her. "Oh, by the way, Alabeth . . ."

"Yes?"

"See that Charles Allister is on your list. We must pair him off with Jillian!"

Alabeth laughed and Octavia went on out, but as the outer door closed, the smile faded a little from Alabeth's face. A flaw in Robert's character which would have emerged sooner or later, whether Piers Castleton had been there or not? No, Octavia was wrong, the flaw had emerged *because* Piers had been there. . . .

6

Jillian emerged from her room in time for a light luncheon of wine and wafers, but it was soon obvious that her morning of seclusion had left her in a stormy mood, for she was determined not to show enthusiasm for anything at all. Alabeth tried to behave as if the previous day had not happened, hoping that this gesture of peace would be received in the manner with which it was offered, but all fell on stony ground. A discussion about which invitations to accept and which names to place on various lists was conducted in a stilted manner which made the whole conversation impossible, and Alabeth gave up long before any mention was made of what arrangements Jillian would like for her own ball. The only time a flicker of interest entered Jillian's blue eyes was at the mention of Octavia's ball and the fact that Count Adam Zaleski would play there for the first time in England.

In desperation Alabeth decided to order the landau for an afternoon drive in Hyde Park, and so at the appointed hour of four the two sisters drove out to join the fashionable throng parading there. It was a beautiful day, perfect late-spring weather, and the air was filled with the scent of flowers and young leaves. The sun shone down from a clear blue sky and there was a lighthearted atmosphere in the capital as England set about enjoying this first peacetime summer for many years, but in the Earl of Wallborough's elegant carriage the atmosphere was anything but lighthearted.

Jillian wasn't smiling, although even Alabeth could tell that she was finding it an effort to remain so sulky. Really she was being very tiresome and difficult, determined to keep the feud simmering at all costs. She looked quite enchanting in her fresh white muslin gown and rose pelisse, the front edges of which were perfectly frilled, and her face was framed by a straw country bonnet tied on with a gauze scarf. Her golden curls were fluffy and there was something quite captivating about her, as the admiring glances of a number of young gentlemen gave proof. For Alabeth's benefit, Jillian kept her eyes lowered, but she could not help glancing up coquettishly now and then, being a natural flirt and unable to resist practicing her wiles on every personable man to catch her eye.

Alabeth felt quite low-spirited, although she managed to hide the fact behind a smiling exterior, for nothing would have let her reveal to Jillian how much the atmosphere was reaching her. She attracted her fair share of attention, for she looked very fetching in a lemon lawn gown, an embroidered mustard spencer, and a yellow chip hat, her hair dressed so that a heavy red ringlet tumbled down over one shoulder. A pagoda parasol twirled behind her, its silken fringe trembling to the motion of the carriage.

"I say! Alabeth!" A man was hailing her.

She turned toward the sound, and her face broke into a warm smile as she saw Charles Allister and a companion riding swiftly toward the landau, but her smile faltered as they came closer and she saw that the companion was Sir Piers Castleton.

Charles was a pale, slender young man, his looks more those of a poet than of a man of action, and he smiled shyly as he reined in, removing his hat. "I was calling you for some time. I began to think you were cutting me."

"As if I would do that. How are you, Charles?"

"In the pink." His hazel eyes moved to Jillian, the admiration plain. "It's Lady Jillian, is it not?"

Jillian's glance was haughty, but it changed abruptly as Piers reined in next to him. The hauteur melted from her eyes and her lips parted—Alabeth could not tell whether it was with alarm or excitement—and she sat forward, her fingers toying nervously with the strings of her reticule. "Good afternoon, Sir Piers, how good it is to see you again."

Piers nodded. "Good afternoon, Lady Jillian. Chatsworth, was it not?"

She flushed a little. "How flattering that you should remember."

"It would be impossible to forget so lovely a face."

Charles continued to stare at Jillian, almost as if he had never before set eyes on such a vision of loveliness, but his admiration went unrewarded, for Jillian all but ignored him. When Alabeth struggled to effect an introduction, Jillian's acknowledgment was cursory, barely within the bounds of good manners.

Piers looked at Alabeth, his gray eyes almost lazy. "Good afternoon, Lady Alabeth."

"Sir." Her back was stiff and straight and she did not look at him. This was dreadful, her first excursion from the house and straightaway she encountered this man.

Charles cleared his throat, obviously a little out by Jillian's lack of interest. "When did you arrive in Town, Alabeth? I called yesterday, but you had not arrived and Lady Jillian was, regrettably, out calling upon Lady Silchester."

Jillian was still looking at Piers with that strange unease which Alabeth had detected so swiftly; she did not even seem to hear Charles speaking. Alabeth felt a little distracted herself, wondering what lay behind Jillian's reaction and being more than a little dismayed at realizing that Jillian and Piers were acquainted. She smiled nervously at Charles. "I—er, I arrived yesterday evening. I knew you had called, for I found your card. You must come to dinner, I'm giving a party next Thursday—"

"I'd be honored." He smiled at her.

Jillian spoke hurriedly. "Please come, too, Sir Piers."

Alabeth's heart sank, for the last thing she wanted was Piers Castleton as her dinner guest, but she was saved from such embarrassment, for he declined the invitation. "I fear that I am otherwise engaged that evening, Lady Jillian."

"Oh. I—I did not think you were in England, Sir Piers. Were you not going to tour Europe?"

"I believe this peace will be too transitory for any such undertaking to be wise."

Her large eyes searched his dark face for a moment before being lowered, still with that air of flusterment which caused Alabeth more and more unease as the moments passed. There was no mistaking the fact that Jillian was affected by Piers Castleton, no mistaking it at all, for she could not have made it more obvious had she shouted it aloud. Alabeth could not tell anything from Piers' face, but everything about Jillian reminded her of the Captain Francis affair the previous summer; the same bubbling excitement, the same shining eyes, and the same general air of agitation. Alabeth's heart sank lower and lower, for the dreadful possibility was that Jillian had transferred her affections to Piers.

To her relief, at that moment another carriage approached from behind and was unable to pass, so she told her coachman to drive on and Charles and Piers rode off across the park, Jillian watching until they vanished from sight. Alabeth said nothing, for to have mentioned anything now would be to certainly provoke another disagreeable argument, but inwardly she was most disquieted by the whole incident. Jillian's attitude suggested an interest which went beyond a single meeting at Chatsworth—but why had her father not mentioned the fact that Jillian was acquainted with Piers? Alabeth stared blindly ahead, her mind racing. Could this be what the Earl was keeping from her? Could an undesirable liaison between Piers Castleton and Jillian have been the reason for the Earl's determination to have Jillian brought out this year, the year when Piers was believed to be going to Europe? The more Alabeth thought of it, the more convinced she became that this was the case, and the more angry she became that her father had not seen fit to tell her. But perhaps she was mistaken, perhaps she had read far more into the whole incident than there actually was. She kept her voice light when she spoke. "I did not know you were acquainted with Sir Piers."

Jillian looked sharply at her. "I'm not. At least— I've met him once."

"At Chatsworth."

"Yes, there was an autumn ball there last year."

Alabeth said nothing more, but Jillian's replies had not reassured her in any way. There was more to it than merely a meeting at a ball, and Alabeth knew she must find out— although asking Jillian directly was out of the question, for it would be regarded as unwarranted interference, only too similar in vein to the whole Francis business. But how could she find anything out? Her father was on his way to Madras, and communicating with him would take far too long. No, there must be another way. Alabeth's eyes cleared suddenly. Of course, she would write secretly to her father's trusted agent at Wallborough Castle, Mr. Bateman, who was not only the steward but also an old friend. If there was anything to know, then he would know it, and he could be persuaded to tell Alabeth, for whom he had always had a soft spot. Yes, she would write to Mr. Bateman and find out exactly what had gone on after that meeting at Chatsworth.

7

The letter remained unwritten for the rest of that day, however, for Jillian was in the house and there was always the risk that she might see what was being written. The following morning she was to go shopping and Alabeth had every intention of writing then, but before she could do so, there was the somewhat ticklish matter of the menu for the dinner party to attend to.

The Earl of Wallborough was a man of plain taste, liking good, old-fashioned English cooking, especially roast beef, and the cook, Mrs. Bourne, had never ventured into the realms of more exciting dishes. Alabeth was determined not to serve roast beef at her first dinner party in more than two years, but the difficulty was persuading Mrs. Bourne to a similar frame of mind. Alabeth waited in the morning room after breakfast, knowing that it would be no easy matter to achieve the cook's willing cooperation.

Mrs. Bourne was plump, cheerful, and blissfully unaware of the new dishes which were beginning to appear at fashionable dinner parties. Smoothing her crisp white apron, she bobbed a curtsy, her large mobcap wobbling on her frizzy gray hair. "You sent for me, madam?"

"I did indeed. I wish to discuss the menu for the dinner party next Thursday."

"Yes, madam. There will be twelve guests, will there not?"

"Yes."

"Oh, I know exactly how much beef to order for that—"

"Ah. Well, I'm afraid that I do not have beef in mind, Mrs. Bourne."

The cook looked quite astounded. "Not have beef? But the Earl always has beef."

"I know that, Mrs. Bourne, but I do not wish to."

The cook sniffed, straightening a little suspiciously. "Mutton? Pork, perhaps?"

"Turkey—"

"Oh, yes, madam." The cook looked positively relieved.

"—in a cream celery sauce," went on Alabeth. "And while I realize that my father always requested swede with his dinner, Mrs. Bourne, I would prefer never to taste that particular vegetable again, so please exclude it."

The cook's face had fallen. "No swede? And the turkey served in *French* sauce?" She was horrified.

"I do not believe the sauce is French, but I do know that it is very good with turkey and that I wish to serve it next Thursday. I wish the meal to begin with purée of artichokes and to end with *meringues à la crème.*"

Mrs. Bourne looked quite faint. "Not oxtail soup and fruit tart?"

"No."

"But—"

"I realize that my father likes certain dishes which he always expects to see set before him, but that is not my way."

"My roast beef is the finest in England."

"Oh, I'm sure it is, Mrs. Bourne. I just wish to try something else."

"Well, I don't know—" The cook's lips were pressed a little crossly together and her bosom expanded as she took a deep breath.

"The dishes are not too difficult for you, are they?" Alabeth asked lightly, knowing that such a slur on the cook's skills would provoke the required response.

"Too difficult? Too *difficult?* I should say they are not!
I am quite able to produce the menu you require,
madam."

"Oh, good, I'm so glad." Alabeth smiled. "And I know
that my guests will be most appreciative and will wish they
too had such an excellent cook."

Mrs. Bourne was a little mollified. "Well, if these new-
fangled things are what you really want—"

"They are, Mrs. Bourne."

There was a slight sniff. "Very well, madam, I will
attend to your wishes."

"Oh, thank you, Mrs. Bourne."

When the cook had gone, Alabeth heaved a sigh of
relief, for although Mrs. Bourne was extremely set in her
ways and could easily have been offended, she was really
too much of a treasure to risk losing. As it was, Alabeth
had had her way and the cook was now determined to
prove that she could produce dishes as fine as anything at
Carlton House, although she had gone away muttering
darkly about folk having Frenchified notions which had no
place in English kitchens, even if there *was* peace now!

Alabeth smiled, going to the window to look out over
the garden, where the wooden seat beneath the mulberry
tree looked so inviting in the morning sun. She had been
intending to write to the Wallborough's steward, as Jillian
had already gone out to shop in Oxford Street, but suddenly the thought of remaining inside was not at all inviting. Picking up the novel she had begun reading the night
before, she left the house to enjoy an hour or so peacefully
reading in the garden.

She wore a cream muslin gown, its bodice drawn in by
dainty tasseled strings, and its hem dragged across the
newly cut lawn. Her sapphire-blue spencer was left unbuttoned to reveal the gown's delicate pin tucks and the
pearl droplet brooch she liked so much. Her hair was

pinned loosely so that the single large ringlet was once again falling down over her shoulder.

The sun sparkled on the lily pond and she could see the fish darting between the flat leaves floating on the surface. The daffodils and tulips smelled good and it was almost possible to forget that she was in London. She settled herself comfortably, removed the book marker, and began to read.

How many minutes had passed she didn't know, but she was suddenly roused from the book by the recognized sound of Sanderson's tread on the path. She glanced up and saw immediately that the butler looked very disconcerted. "What is it?" she asked.

"Sir Piers Castleton has called, my lady."

She closed the book with a snap. "I am not at home."

"Oh, yes you are, Alabeth," Piers himself said, strolling casually along the path, his silver-handled cane swinging between his gloved fingers. He was dressed quite perfectly, like the Corinthian he was, in a close-fitting corbeau-colored coat and nankeen breeches. The tassels of his Hessian boots swung from side to side as he walked, and the diamond pin in his white cambric cravat flashed in the sunlight as he paused before her, removing his hat and bowing. "Good morning, Alabeth."

"I have no wish to speak to you, sir."

"How unfortunate, for I have every intention of speaking with you."

"Leave immediately or I will have you thrown out."

His gray eyes swept lazily over her and then swung to Sanderson, who looked faint with horror at the thought of being asked to lay hands upon such a gentleman. Piers smiled and then looked at her again. "I think not, Alabeth, especially as I do not intend to take up a great deal of your precious time."

Her cheeks were hot as she felt forced to give way,

nodding to Sanderson that he was dismissed. Clasping her hands in her lap, she looked coldly at Piers. "Well?"

Still smiling, he rested one boot on the seat beside her, leaning forward to look down into her angry eyes. "How very lovely you look, as pretty as a picture in your blue gown, surrounded by spring flowers."

"Please come to the point, sir."

"Are you always as stormy as this, Alabeth?"

"*Lady* Alabeth."

His eyebrow was raised. "So formal? I recall a time when I was Piers to you."

"Those times are long since gone, sir."

"So it seems. Which brings me to the reason for my visit. Am I to take it that your conduct yesterday in Hyde Park was a sample of how you mean to go on?"

"It is, for I certainly do not think you merit anything more."

"Then shame on you, Alabeth Manvers, for your bad manners verged on the vulgar."

Quivering with anger, she rose from the seat. "Don't presume to comment upon my conduct, sirrah," she breathed furiously.

"I will comment as I see fit, madam, for you appear to believe that you may behave as you wish. Well you may not, as I am here to inform you. It was inexcusable yesterday to have issued a dinner invitation to Charles Allister and to have excluded me so pointedly. As a lady of quality, of rank, and fashion, you should have known better, Alabeth. Correctly you should have waited, written the invitation to him and had it delivered, thus avoided the embarrassment of what actually happened. I did not think it would ever fall to me to have to point out the errors of your way, but it has—and here I am."

"How dare you! How dare you come here and insult me!"

"On the contrary, madam, I came here because you insulted me. I have no intention at all of being subjected to such a dismal display of pettiness again.''

She hardly trusted herself to speak. "Please leave," she said, her voice shaking.

"Not until I have a guarantee that from now on the summer will proceed with a little more decorum from you.''

"I will not give you any such guarantee.''

"Very well, then I must issue a warning to you.''

"A warning?''

"That I shall not meekly accept whatever affront you see fit to toss at me.''

"I conduct myself in the only way possible, given what has happened in the past.''

He searched her face for a moment. "You may give thanks that you are a woman, Alabeth, for I would not endure such churlishness from a man.''

"It is hardly churlishness.''

"Oh, but it is, and I think you know it.''

She looked away, unable to meet his piercing gaze. "Please leave," she said again.

"You still refuse to moderate your behavior toward me in public?''

"I do," she replied, feeling very hot and uncomfortable before his steady eyes.

"Oh, how challenging you are, Alabeth," he said softly, "and I was never a man to refuse a challenge. Consider the gauntlet picked up and be on your guard from now on, for I no longer promise to turn the other cheek to your insults.''

"What you do is immaterial to me.''

"Is that really so?" He smiled a little. "I think not; I think it matters very much to you what I do and where I am.''

"You flatter yourself.''

"No, Alabeth. I just know you very well indeed.''

"You may have known me once, sir. That is certainly no longer the case." She turned away sharply. "I have asked you to leave."

"So you have, but there is one thing more . . ."

"Yes?"

"Have you seen Zaleski yet?"

Baffled by this sudden change of subject, she turned back to face him. "I beg your pardon?"

"Count Adam Zaleski, have you seen him yet?"

"No. Why?"

"Because I think you may be in for something of a shock, Alabeth."

She stared at him. "I don't understand . . ."

"You will, the moment you see him—at Octavia Seaham's ball, I believe. I think you will wish you had remained in Charterleigh."

Her green eyes moved slowly over his face. "I wish that anyway, sir."

He smiled. "No doubt. Good day, Alabeth."

"Sir."

She watched him walk away, wondering what he had meant when he had talked of the Count. She was conscious that she was trembling still, and she sat down, automatically picking up her book, but the pages swam blindly before her and she closed it again, glancing back along the path where he had gone.

The curiosity she had felt at his remarks about the Count faded into the background, and anger stirred again in her breast. Let him threaten what he would, she would not temper her conduct in the slightest, for he merited everything he received at her hands. Please let it not be that Jillian had formed an attachment for him, for that would be too dreadful to countenance. She lowered her eyes, angry with herself then, for not once during the time he had been with her had she thought of saying anything to him about Jillian. She should have done so; she should have informed him that she expected him to stay well away from her sister, over whom she had total charge.

Suddenly she stood up again; she could no longer delay writing to Wallborough. As she entered the house, she called Sanderson.

"Yes, my lady?"

"I wish to write a letter."

"I will bring the materials immediately, my lady."

She returned to the morning room, where it was still sunny, and a minute or so later the butler was setting out the paper, inkstand, and quills. Alone again, she sat at the table. How did one write discreetly that one suspected one's father of not telling the entire truth and one's sister of maybe conducting a clandestine affair with an unsuitable gentleman? Pensively she drew the quill through her fingers, gazing at the gleaming silver inkstand, and then at last she dipped the quill in the ink and began to write.

Dear Mr. Bateman,

Forgive me for writing such an unusual letter to you, and please understand that my only anxiety is to be careful in attending to my duties as my sister's guardian. I know that I may safely communicate with you as you are an old and trusted friend. As you are no doubt aware, I have charge of my sister this summer, but I am troubled that there is something which I have not been told, something which most probably occurred while she was at Wallborough. I fear that a certain gentleman's name may be involved, the same gentleman whose appearance at Charterleigh caused so much upset several years ago. I realize that I may be asking you to break my father's confidence, but my position is rendered very difficult by not being in full possession of the facts. Please understand that my father will never hear of any reply you may give me. I will certainly destroy any communication, for I would not wish to jeopardize your situation in any way. Forgive me again for involving you in my predicament.

I am, yours very sincerely,

Alabeth Manvers

She read the letter again, pondering the steward's reaction when he received it. She could see him now, a comfortable, rather untidy man complete with a rather dilapidated gray-powdered wig and clay pipe, sitting back in his enormous high-backed chair in the kitchen at the home farm. He was indeed an old and trusted friend, and she knew in her heart that if he knew anything at all concerning Jillian, he would respond to this appeal.

She folded the letter and then held the sealing wax to a candle flame. The thick wax dripped onto the paper and a moment later she was pressing her seal ring into the soft surface. There, it was done now—it would be taken by the letter carrier that very afternoon and would reach Derbyshire in a day or so. She hated going behind people's backs in this way, but Jillian's present attitude made any other course impossible, and after the business of Captain Francis, Alabeth knew she did not dare to take any chance where her hasty, romantically inclined sister was concerned.

The grave misgivings she had felt that night at Charterleigh when she had at last given in to her father's wishes returned to her now as she placed the letter in the silver dish in the vestibule. You should have refused, Alabeth Manvers, she told herself, you should have refused. . . .

8

Mrs. Bourne came up trumps for the dinner party, producing a meal which all the guests pronounced to be superb. For Alabeth, too, it was something of a triumph, as it was her first venture into entertaining since Robert's death and it had been important to her that it went well. Jillian was perhaps a little restrained still, but she abstained from being too difficult and her manner was put down to shyness rather than willfulness.

Sometime before midnight the majority of guests departed, leaving only Octavia, Charles Allister, and the rather elderly bachelor Lord Gainsford. They sat comfortably in the drawing room, enjoying a liqueur with walnuts and raisins, and the great windows stood open to let in the cool night air. The smell of the plane trees wafted in from the square, together with the sound of occasional laughter from the direction of Gunter's, where a number of people had adjourned after the theater. The drawing room was a magnificent chamber, its walls hung with red silk and its ceiling a marvelous confection of gilt plasterwork, scrolls and leaves, lozenges, and spirals. On the floor was a Kidderminster carpet, woven especially to echo the ceiling design, and the whole thing was set off to perfection by the furniture upholstered in dark-ruby velvet. Dominating everything was a white marble and ormolu fireplace, a prime example of Adam's genuis, and in the corners of the room stood particularly handsome candle stands, their metalwork gleaming in the soft light.

Octavia sat comfortably on a shield-back chair, glancing

appreciatively around. "This is a beautiful room, Alabeth, I find it quite perfect."

"My father would be delighted to hear you say so."

"No doubt, which is why I would never tell him." Octavia chuckled.

"You are quite incorrigible," she replied, smiling.

Lord Gainsford nodded, his white wig leaving a dusting of powder on his otherwise impeccable black velvet shoulder. "Always were a regular wretch, Octavia, takin' great delight in makin' a fellow's life a misery."

The Duchess beamed, smoothing her russet taffeta skirts. "You had your chance Gainsford, but you missed it and let me marry Seaham instead."

"M'dear, I couldn't afford you; you'd have made a beggar of me inside a month."

Octavia's eyes were speculative. "I wonder what sort of go we'd have made of it? I admit to always liking that wicked look in your eyes; it promised all manner of entertaining things."

He flushed a little and cleared his throat. "Not in front of the little gel, Octavia, it ain't done!" He glanced at Jillian.

Octavia smiled again. "Come, now, I've said nothing to make Jillian blush, have I, my dear?"

Jillian shook her head. "No, of course not."

"You're looking quite delightful tonight—isn't she, Gainsford?"

"Yes, quite devastating. You remind me of my dear sister, for she was an exquisite little thing too."

Octavia pursed her lips wickedly. "Your sister always said you were a tyrant, never letting her live her own life and vetting every single beau who had the temerity to come calling."

"It's a fellow's duty to see his sister comes to no grief, and I did well enough for her, got her a Marquis."

Octavia looked even more wicked. "She said you were a

tyrant, and when I realized that your name was on Alabeth's list tonight, I simply couldn't resist placing a great deal of money on a certain nag in the Derby."

"What nag?"

"Why, Tyrant, of course!" Octavia was almost hugging herself with glee.

Charles tore his eyes away from Jillian to look at Octavia. "The horse has never won anything in its life; I've even heard tell it has a wooden leg."

Octavia was unruffled. "The creature will not dare to lose for me, especially as I am celebrating the King's birthday the next day."

Lord Gainsford was smiling. "Well, I wish you well, Octavia, although I can't say I approve of ladies involving themselves in gambling."

"Don't be so pompous," she retorted. "Besides this isn't gambling, it's backing a certainty."

"I suppose you are in with a knowing one?"

"With the Duke of Grafton himself, to say nothing of the jockey, Frank Buckle. They inform me that Tyrant cannot fail, and I believe them. I shall be there myself to cheer the brute home."

Jillian was shocked. "You are going to the Derby, Your Grace?"

"Why, yes, I wouldn't miss it, Epson has the most *iniquitous* EO and faro tables!"

"But don't they also have fairs and crowds of the most disreputable sort?" asked Jillian, obviously shocked that a lady of such high rank should be attending so vulgar and popular a race meeting.

Octavia chuckled again. "Of course they do, my dear. There are similar crowds at Ascot, only there they masquerade as high society. You'll see for yourself when you join my house party for Ascot week."

"Are we joining you?" Jillian glanced uncertainly at Alabeth, who nodded.

"Why, yes, Octavia has kindly asked us to be her guests at Stoneleigh Park, which is barely a mile from Ascot racecourse."

Lord Gainsford beckoned a footman to refill his glass. "I don't know what the world's coming to," he grumbled. "This damned Peace of Amiens has sent the whole world mad, completely mad. There's more money being squandered on leisure and pleasure this summer than ever before, and all because people are foolish enough to believe Bonaparte to be sincere."

Jillian was fearful that the conversation would turn upon the boring topic of the First Consul's political machinations, and she hastily intervened. "Well, at least the peace means that Count Adam Zaleski will be coming to Town."

Lord Gainsford nodded. "Aye, a pretty fellow from all accounts, guaranteed to have all the ladies swooning at the sight of him."

"What is he like?" asked Alabeth. "Has anyone here seen him yet? Octavia?"

"No," replied the Duchess. "Like Gainsford, I only know what is said of him. He's reputed to be quite the most divine of creatures, all golden and angelic, and yet full of Polish fire. Why do you ask? Have you heard something interesting?"

Alabeth lowered her eyes. "No."

"You've aroused my curiosity—"

"It's nothing, truly it isn't."

Jillian warmed to the subject of the Count. "I simply can't wait to see him."

Charles was scornful. "I'm given to understand that he's nothing more than a salon musician, a little gaudy, and reliant upon his looks to carry him through."

Jillian's eyes flashed with annoyance and Octavia reproved him a little. "Nonsense, Charles, you don't know what you're talking about. I have it on most reliable evidence that he is indeed a virtuoso of the first order and can bring forth more life from the pianoforte than anyone else in the world.''

Charles was determined to be unimpressed, and Alabeth knew that it was because he was jealous of Jillian's interest in the Count, for he went on, ''I trust you are right, Octavia, for I am already heartily sick and tired of hearing the fellow's name. Zaleski, Zaleski, Zaleski, that's all one hears from morning till night, in every drawing room, club, or pleasure garden.''

Jillian was superior. ''And you will continue to hear of him, sir, because he is a genius, a veritable magician of music, and I pray with all my heart that I will be fortunate enough to be one of his pupils.'' She looked at Octavia. ''He *is* still going to give tuition, isn't he, Your Grace?''

''I believe so.''

Lord Gainsford eyed Jillian for a moment. ''I presume, then, that you are a talented player yourself, Lady Jillian.''

''I play a little,'' she said, flushing prettily and with a genuine modesty, which probably made Charles Allister even more wretchedly her slave than he already was.

''Then I don't know whether I should advise you to seek tuition from the Count,'' said the old lord, smiling at her, ''for he is said to be most unorthodox, thinking nothing of playing a black key with his thumb, or of crossing a longer finger over a shorter one.''

Jillian was nonplussed that anyone of such stature could disregard the basic rules. ''Surely you are wrong, sir.''

''I believe that that is how he achieves such fluency, but what he can master so effortlessly would surely be impossible for lesser mortals. I gather that his own compositions are so diabolically difficult that another fellow attempting to emulate him was well advised to have an eminent surgeon at hand to attend the finger damage which resulted.''

Octavia and Alabeth laughed, Jillian looked primly disapproving of such criticism of her idol, and Charles looked baleful, obviously despising the handsome Count well in advance.

Lord Gainsford chuckled a little and then smiled kindly at Jillian. "I am teasing you, m'dear, so don't take me seriously. I have always liked to hear a pretty gal playing the pianoforte, so will you indulge me a little and play for us now?"

"Oh, I don't know . . ."

Charles was brighter suddenly. "Please do, Lady Jillian."

"If you would really like to hear me . . ."

The two gentlemen stood immediately, Lord Gainsford managing somehow to offer her his arm first. "Of course we would, m'dear, it would be the perfect end of an excellent evening."

Alabeth and Octavia commandeered Charles between them, the Duchess chiding him just a little as they ascended to the music room some way behind Jillian and Lord Gainsford. "Do smile a little, Charles, for you look so gloomy that I fear poor Alabeth will think she has lost her touch as a hostess."

He was aghast. "Oh, please, Alabeth, never think that."

"I shall if you continue to frown."

"You both know why I'm frowning."

"We do indeed," Octavia replied firmly, "and I, for one, think you're going about it all the wrong way."

"I'm not a beau. I haven't got the wiles of a skilled lover," he grumbled.

"No, you're just moping around with spaniel eyes, and it ain't the way with a minx like young Jillian," said Octavia. "Ignore her a little, it will do her good."

They entered the music room, where an alert Sanderson had already placed some candles, and Jillian took her place at the pianoforte and began to play. The beautiful notes of a Mozart minuet stole out into the silent room, her delicate little fingers moving softly and expertly over the keys. The performance was faultless, the work of someone who was already very accomplished.

She smiled with justifiable pleasure when they all applauded her afterward, although her smile froze a little when Charles made so bold as to take her hand and raise it to her lips. She was not interested in him and she showed it in the way she coolly removed her hand, her eyes flickering on to smile at Lord Gainsford, who was most effusive with his praise. Octavia frowned a little at Jillian's conduct, especially when she saw how low the snub had brought poor Charles.

He went to where Alabeth was standing by the window. "Oh, Charles, I'm so sorry—" she began.

But he was suddenly and surprisingly firm. "She is the one for me, Alabeth, and I'm set upon winning her."

"Nothing would please me more than to welcome you as my brother-in-law, Charles, but I cannot say that I have seen anything encouraging in her manner toward you."

He smiled a little ruefully. "Nor I, but I must try, for I have never before felt this way."

Alabeth glanced at Jillian as she rose from the stool and once again took Lord Gainsford's arm. "I wish you well, Charles," she said softly, "but I swear she does not deserve you."

"She is the most perfect of creatures," he breathed, unable to take his eyes off Jillian as she left the room on Lord Gainsford's arm. "I adore her with all my heart and know that there is no other bride for me."

Alabeth said nothing more, but she felt very sad, for she was sure that Charles was destined for nothing but heartbreak, for Jillian was completely indifferent to him.

9

On the third of June, the Duke of Grafton's horse Tyrant won the Derby with great ease, and Octavia returned in triumph from Epsom, not only having picked the winner but also having scored a notable success at an EO table. After such an excellent day, she had no doubt at all that her ball would be similarly memorable, as indeed it was.

The day dawned sweet and clear, and as it was the King's birthday, the carriages thronging London's streets were decorated with sprays of flowers, the coachmen and footmen adorning their hats with similar sprays. There was only one cloud on Octavia's horizon, and that was the fact that she was summoned to Court during the afternoon, and this necessitated an unfashionable step back in time of nearly fifty years, the King and Queen always insisting that hooped skirts, high headdresses, painted faces, and a great many diamonds were the only suitable fashion for such an occasion. Octavia had squeezed herself into the obligatory sedan chair, her skirts folded around her and her head bowed to protect the ridiculously high confection of wig and feathers, and she had been borne to St. James's, feeling excessively conspicuous, for she attracted too much unwelcome attention from the vulgar—usually an unbridled mirth which made her fume at the monarchs' refusal to move with the times. However, the ordeal behind her, she returned to Seaham House and the preparations for the ball began in earnest.

At the Wallborough house in Berkeley Square things were a great deal quieter, neither Alabeth nor Jillian having any other engagements before the ball. Alabeth had kept a wary eye on Jillian, but nothing untoward had occurred and there had, mercifully, been no other encounters with Piers Castleton. Jillian had conducted herself with reasonable decorum, although her manner toward poor Charles Allister was still cool and offhand. Only one thing caused Alabeth some alarm, and that was the receipt of a brief note from the steward at Wallborough, informing her that he would come up to London at the first opportunity as he had something to communicate to her which he would prefer not to set down on paper. This served to confirm to Alabeth that she had been right to be suspicious, and it made her very guarded where Jillian's movements were concerned, that young lady frequently complaining that she doubted if anyone else in Town was being subjected to such rigorous rules and regulations. Alabeth knew she was being a little too strict and tried very hard to relax, but it was really very difficult when she found herself thinking time and time again of the Captain Francis affair and how Jillian had deliberately thwarted the basic rules of behavior in order to be with him. Jillian seemed to be behaving herself, however, obviously determined not to provoke Alabeth into refusing to go to the ball and thus preclude any chance of seeing the great Zaleski play.

The Count's arrival in Town had been greeted with a great flurry of excitement among the ladies, reports reaching Alabeth of his incredible good looks and charming manners. He was declared to be quite irresistible and was the object of much adoration, it being the ambition of a large number of ladies to secure him as a lover. Alabeth listened to all this a little skeptically, finding it hard to believe that any one man could be quite so devastating, but she did wonder about him, remembering Piers Castleton's enigmatic warning.

The hour was approaching when they were due to leave for Seaham House, and Alabeth was waiting in the drawing room for Jillian. She stood by the window, gazing out over the twilit square where the leaves on the plane trees were almost motionless in the calm of the summer evening. She wore a silver muslin gown picked out with tiny flowers embroidered in black, and a large, soft ostrich plume curled down from her jeweled hair. Black beads shimmered on her elegant shawl and there were rubies at her throat and in her ears. Her only other adornment was her wedding ring, worn outside her elbow-length white gloves. She was conscious of a feeling of nervous anticipation, for although she had attended many functions, this was the first one where practically all the *ton* would be present. It was also Jillian's first London ball, the first occasion at which she would be properly on display, to be commented upon, gauged, assessed . . .

She turned as she heard Jillian's light steps approaching, and then she was there, a vision in peach, her silver slippers peeping out beneath her hem and a beautiful pearl-studded comb drawing her soft, curly hair behind one ear. Her excitement was infectious, for her lips were parted just a little and her blue eyes were lustrous and shining as she twirled, all antagonism forgotten for a moment as she displayed her gown for her sister to admire. "How do I look?"

"Exquisite."

"Truly?"

Alabeth smiled. "Truly. You will set them all at sixes and sevens."

Jillian almost hugged herself with delight, but then she seemed to remember that she was at odds with Alabeth, and her smile faded. Her voice became more sedate and her glance was more cool. "Shall we go, then?"

Alabeth could not help but be conscious of the chill which pushed the warmth aside, but she affected not to notice. "Yes, of course, I believe I hear the landau outside."

The hoods of the carriage were down on such a warm, still evening, and they sat side by side, Jillian becoming more and more nervous and excited as they neared Seaham House. There were carriages converging on that one address from all directions, and the evening was noisy with the sound of hooves and wheels. Seaham House itself was ablaze with lights, every window brilliant and not a single curtain drawn. Countless colored lanterns decorated the elegant facade and the steps beneath the portico were strewn with moss and flowers, placed with care to look as if they grew there. Garlands of greenery were draped around the Corinthian columns, and servants carrying flambeaux hurried out to greet each carriage as it arrived.

The landau joined the long queue, for it was taking some time for each vehicle to be escorted to the foot of the steps, the guests to alight, and the carriage to move on to make room for the next one. Jillian did not notice at all, and it was some time before Alabeth noticed, but fate had placed them directly behind Piers Castleton's barouche. She watched the servants, flambeaux smoking and fluttering as they escorted the barouche the final yards to the house. The carriage door was flung open and Piers alighted.

He was very correct in black velvet, pausing for a moment to adjust the white frill protruding from his cuff before turning to accept his gloves from a footman. His white shirt and stiff cravat looked very startling in the half-light, and his disheveled hair gave just the right hint of nonchalance to an otherwise formal appearance. Alabeth watched him, silently acknowledging that whatever her opinion of him, she could not deny that he was incredibly handsome—but then, that was one thing she had never denied.

He passed on into the house, from which the strains of music emerged into the open air, and then the flambeaux were bobbing beside the Wallborough landau and Jillian was almost on the edge of her seat as she stared at the magnificent decorations covering the front of Seaham House.

Inside, the decorations were no less magnificent, for Octavia had certainly made free with the Duke's purse. In the flower-strewn vestibule each lady was presented with a tiny wrist bouquet of exotic flowers, obviously picked from the hothouses at Stoneleigh Park, and there were fountains playing endlessly into artificial pools where the flashing forms of gold and silver fish could be seen. Octavia had surpassed herself, more than earning her reputation as London's premier hostess, for one doubted that Devonshire House or Melbourne House could have come up to this lavish display.

The Duke and Duchess waited at the foot of the great marble steps leading down into the immense, glittering ballroom, the Duke looking somewhat gloomy, for he was pining for the ample charms of Lady Adelina Carver, who was causing him some anxiety because of her expressed preference for Harry Ponsonby. The thought that perhaps at this very moment she was languishing in Ponsonby's arms was making the Duke very tetchy indeed. He loathed having to do his duty at the best of times, but tonight was finding it more irksome than ever.

Beside him, Octavia was resplendent in a vivid jade-green satin which was picked out with hundreds of tiny sequins. Knowing full well her spouse's despondent thoughts, she felt no sympathy whatsoever, feeling that he merited none because of his frequent and open excursions outside the marriage bed.

The master of ceremonies, very imposing in the Seaham livery of maroon and gold, stepped forward as Alabeth and Jillian approached, and his cane rapped loudly on the marble floor as he called out their names. A great many faces were turned immediately in their direction, quizzing glasses were raised, and there were whispers behind fans, for the Earl of Wallborough's beautiful daughters were the object of considerable interest. Many remembered only too well the scandal which had centered upon Alabeth six years before, and now they wondered if Jillian was a similar chip off the Wallborough block. But for every slightly unkind soul, there was another who welcomed them with genuine pleasure, for whatever Alabeth may have done in the past, she had still been a very popular young lady, whose true friends would have forgiven her almost anything, especially a romantic, if undesirable, match with a charming rake like Lord Manvers.

Alabeth began to descend the steps, Jillian following slightly behind, and Octavia came to meet them, smiling with delight. "My dears, you both look delectable, quite delectable. Is that not so, sir?" She nudged her morose husband.

"Eh? Oh, yes—yes, the evening goes very well."

His wife frowned. "Do pay attention sir, for already you have asked the Marquis of Fullsdon how his wife is, and the world knows she has left him."

Alabeth smothered a smile, for Octavia's words conjured up quite an entertaining picture. The Duke scowled, muttering that Fullsdon was such a miserly wretch he was surprised his very hounds hadn't left him too. Octavia looked cross, but then forgot him as she linked arms with Alabeth and drew her aside. "I do not think a single soul has not accepted for tonight," she said with ill-concealed delight. "I could not be more pleased, truly I couldn't."

"I'm glad for you, Octavia, for you've worked very hard, and everything looks most exquisite."

Octavia looked satisfied as she gazed across the crowded floor, which had been thoroughly sanded and decorated with the stenciled shapes of stars and half-moons. Beneath the dazzling chandeliers, jeweled ladies and velvet-clad gentlemen moved to the sweet music of a cotillion, and at the far end of the floor was the orchestra's dais. To one side stood the pianoforte which Count Adam Zaleski was to play a little later.

Alabeth glanced at the pianoforte. "Has the Count arrived yet?"

"Naturally, for I do not promise such tidbits and then not produce them."

"What is he like?"

Octavia hesitated. "He is very handsome," she replied, glancing very swiftly at Alabeth's eyes and then away again.

"And?"

"What do you mean?"

"Come, now, Octavia, I can tell that there is more than just that."

"Well, my dear, it's—" Octavia broke off with some relief as the master of ceremonies announced more guests. "I simply must go now, Alabeth," she said swiftly, her satin skirts swishing as she hurried back to join the Duke.

Alabeth watched her curiously. There *was* something strange about this Count Zaleski—but what could it be? She put the Count from her thoughts then as she glanced around looking for Jillian, only to see her surrounded by an admiring group of young gentlemen, all eager to claim her for a dance. It was obvious that she was set to be a resounding success, for not only was she young and beautiful, she was also the daughter of the Earl of Wallborough and therefore most definitely a catch.

Alabeth herself attracted a similar amount of attention, for she possessed the same assets, with the added bonus of being a widow owning the considerable Manvers fortune. For the next hour or so she enjoyed herself, dancing with a succession of partners, receiving a great many compliments, and feeling very much the honey to all the bees.

She had forgotten Piers Castleton, but she remembered him very sharply indeed when, after a brief intermission, the orchestra struck up again and she happened to glance at the floor and see that he was Jillian's partner. They made a very handsome pair and Jillian danced so very well, but the adoration on her face was only too apparent and could not but be commented on. Alabeth was dismayed at such an unguarded display, and she knew that already a number of people had remarked it and were watching. Oh, Jillian, *Jillian,* why can't you be more discreet? Helplessly, Alabeth watched, but if she could find fault with Jillian's conduct, she could certainly not say the same of Piers', for there was nothing untoward in his manner at all; he was simply partnering Jillian in a dance. But what was he really thinking? What was really in the glance of those dark, inscrutable eyes?

The dance ended and Alabeth was about to hurry toward her sister, when her attention was taken up with a rather large, elderly, army officer, his scarlet dress uniform bristling with medals and decorations. "Lady Alabeth? D'you remember me? Fitzwilliam, General Sir John Fitzwilliam." He bowed.

She wanted to speak to Jillian, but etiquette demanded that she stop to speak with the General first. From the corner of her eye she saw Jillian and Piers strolling off the floor and entering the adjoining room, where refreshments were being served. Smiling brightly at the General, she held out her hand. "Of course I remember you, Sir John, you are Robert's great-uncle."

"Damned sorry affair, that duel."

"Yes."

"Still, it's past now, and I'm pleased to see you back in circulation, my dear, and looking as magnificent as ever."

"You are too kind, sir."

"Nonsense, you're the best-looking woman here, and that includes your pretty little sister. Will you make an old man very proud by taking some refreshment with him?" He offered her his arm.

She wanted to refuse, for she saw that Jillian and Piers had reemerged, having only gone for some iced champagne, but to have refused the General would have

been the height of rudeness and Alabeth could no more
have hurt his feelings than she could have flown. Smiling,
she slipped her hand over his arm and they proceeded
toward the refreshment room. Her dismay deepened a little
when she saw Jillian put her glass on a table and smile at
Piers, stepping with him onto the floor to dance once
again. Really, it was too bad of them both—Piers no
longer being blameless—for they both knew that it was inadvisable for a young lady at her first ball to spend so
much time exclusively with the same partner.

Jillian deliberately avoided catching Alabeth's eyes, but
Piers showed no concern, coolly inclining his head, which
made Alabeth all the more angry with him.

In the refreshment room the general inquired which dish
Alabeth would like to sample, and she surveyed the white-
clothed tables lining the side of the room. Each one was
laid out with succulent delicacies, from pies and tarts to
cold viands, from salads and cheese to magnificent hot-
house peaches, and there were ices so cold and firm that
they were surely a miracle on such a hot night. Under
normal circumstances, she would have liked a sample of
nearly everything, but such was her anger with Jillian and
Piers that she had little appetite, settling for one of the
delicious ices. The general was attentive and charming, and
in spite of her feelings, she found herself enjoying his
rather old-fashioned company.

Jillian continued to do her best to avoid her sister's disapproving eye, and was by now causing quite a stir among
the other guests as she danced for a third time with Piers.
Alabeth felt very low indeed, remembering only too clearly
how the Earl had frowned upon Jillian becoming
acquainted with gentlemen like Piers. What *would* he say
had he been here now?

Glancing around, she saw that there were raised fans
concealing whispering lips, and quizzing glasses directed at
Jillian, who danced on, seeming quite oblivious to the *faux*

pas of which she was guilty. Alabeth knew that something would have to be done, or her foolish sister would have no reputation left, and this at the very first London ball she had attended.

The dance came to an end at last, and Alabeth moved resolutely forward to speak to Jillian, but fate was determined to thwart her plans, for there was a loud drumroll and the master of ceremonies announced that the moment had arrived: the Count was to play for them. A great stir of anticipation ran through the gathering and everyone pressed forward to be as close to the pianoforte as possible.

Jillian's gasp of excitement was almost audible to Alabeth, who watched as she hurried forward, her peach-colored skirts rustling. Jillian was determined to be as close as possible to this man she idolized, even though she only knew of him from what she had heard and read. Charles Allister watched her progress with an even more gloomy expression on his normally cheerful face. Remaining where he was, he leaned against a column and looked as if he were praying that the Count would at least fall off his stool, or maybe play a thousand wrong notes.

Alabeth moved slowly to the entrance of the refreshment room, her heart beating more swiftly, although she could not have said exactly why. Something made her refrain from joining the rest of the audience. Her hand rested against the gilded carving of the doorjamb as she gazed across the heads of the gathering at the pianoforte. An expectant hush fell over everyone, and she could see the eager, almost unbearable anticipation on Jillian's face, and then at last the Count appeared from the side entrance of the ballroom, a tall, slender figure in dark blue, stepping up lightly toward the dais.

Alabeth's heart almost stopped, and her trembling fingers crept hesitantly to touch the ruby necklace at her throat. Seeing him was like looking upon a ghost . . . the ghost of Robert, Lord Manvers. . . .

10

He was tall and, like Robert, managed to look at once highly fashionable and elegant, and yet gave an air of indifference to his appearance. His face was finely boned, and he could indeed have almost been described as beautiful, and yet there was something extremely virile and arresting about him, from the flash of his passionate blue eyes to the slight curve of his knowing lips. Everything about him reminded her of Robert; the same golden hair and blue eyes, the same graceful movements, and the same romantic aura which hinted so subtly at the controlled fire lying just beneath the surface. She gazed at him, mixed emotions sweeping over her as painful memories were stirred. But he wasn't Robert, she told herself, he was Count Adam Zaleski, the exiled Polish nobleman who was now the darling of Paris and who was all set at this one splendid occasion to become London's darling too.

The hush was so intense as he took his seat at the pianoforte that truly a pin could have been heard to drop, and all eyes were directed at the slender man whose pale fingers were poised above the keys. The first soft notes stole out over the audience and immediately they were held spellbound by an enchanting touch which was full of poetry, fire, and soul. His playing was so delicate and sensuous that with a single note he could express a whole range of nuances, and the expression on his face was one of deep concentration: he was oblivious to his audience, so completely was he lost in the music. The pianoforte came to a strange life of its own, so intense and magnificent that it sent shivers of delight through the audience, and like everyone else there, Alabeth could not take her eyes from him.

Jillian, who had perhaps awaited this moment with more eagerness than anyone else, was transfixed by his mastery. She could only gaze in wonderment, wishing that such glorious music could flow from her fingers too. Charles watched for a while, but then suddenly turned and walked away, his steps inaudible above the musical eloquence of the man at the pianoforte.

Quite suddenly, it seemed, the Count had finished and had begun to rise from the stool. For a breathless moment the bewitched silence continued, and then there was rapturous applause as everyone showed their complete appreciation of his genius. He smiled a little, his blue eyes sweeping over the delighted faces before him. London was his, and he had conquered it with music.

Alabeth alone did not applaud; she was still shocked into immobility by the strong resemblance he bore to Robert, but at last she tore her eyes away and turned a little to find herself staring straight at Piers Castleton, who had been watching her for some time. He knew what she was thinking; he had known all along, and that was why he had said she would perhaps have been better off remaining at Charterleigh.

For the first time she became aware of the curious glances of several other people, for they too had noted the Pole's resemblance to the late Lord Manvers, and she took a hold of herself then, not wishing to convey her innermost thoughts to the world at large. Holding her head up, she turned back into the refreshment room, but her heart was thundering still and her hand trembled as she sipped her glass of iced champagne.

Several minutes passed, filled with the sound of excited conversation from the ballroom as everyone strove to be presented to the Count, but then the orchestra struck up yet another cotillion and gradually the ball returned to something approaching normality. People began to drift back into the refreshment room and Alabeth began to feel a little more mistress of herself—until she heard Octavia hailing her and turned to see her advancing on the Count's arm.

"Alabeth, my dear," said Octavia, smiling and yet looking a little uncomfortable as she had obviously noted earlier how like Robert he was, "the Count wishes to be presented to you."

"To me?" Alabeth's green eyes widened, fleeing momentarily to his face. How warm and speculative his glance was.

Octavia's fan wafted busily to and fro. "Count Adam Zaleski, may I introduce you to Lady Alabeth Manvers. Alabeth, Count Zaleski." Octavia was obviously disconcerted by the situation, the undertones of which may have escaped the Count but certainly had not escaped a great many others, who were wondering what effect he was having upon Lord Manvers' beautiful widow.

His eyes were dark and burning as he bowed to her, taking her hand and raising it to his lips. *"Enchanté, madame,"* he murmured.

She sank into a curtsy. "Sir."

"Lady Alabeth, will you honor me by being my first dancing partner here in England?" His voice was soft and his English excellent, although spoken with a heavy Polish accent.

"I think, sir, that the honor will be mine," she replied.

"Oh, no," he murmured, his fingers firm around her. "Never yours, my lady, only mine, I promise you that."

She was in something of a daze as she walked with him into the ballroom, conscious of the envious gaze of many of the ladies, who would have given their eyeteeth to be in her place now. The dance was slow and stately, but it provided him with many opportunities to speak to her, and he did not waste one of them. She was flattered by his obvious admiration, and was not a little attracted to him, but perhaps that was because of the ghost she saw gazing from his ardent eyes. There was something very compelling about him, a continual suggestion of a passionate desire held just in check by a highly civilized veneer. He was possessed of all the fire and emotion of his nation, and yet imbued with the elegant refinement of the French, and the mixture was very potent indeed. She was too aware not only of how dangerously attractive he was, but also of how very sure he was of himself. He had undoubtedly made countless conquests, and the desire in his glance promised that he fully intended to conquer her too.

The dance ended, but he continued to hold her hand, drawing her a little nearer than necessary. "My lady, I hope that we will meet again . . . soon."

She drew her hand away. "No doubt we will, sir."

"I must have your promise, for nothing less will do."

"Please, sir." She glanced around in some embarrassment, conscious of the interest they were attracting as they stood alone in the center of the floor.

"You will dance with me again?" he asked.

"I could not be so selfish, sir, for there are a great many ladies who desire very much to dance with you."

His lazy smile struck right through her, an echo from the past. "Then I must be content, my lady," he said softly, "for at least I have been fortunate enough to meet England's most beautiful lady."

"Are you always this gallant and attentive, sir?"

"Only when beauty commands, and it has commanded me from the moment I saw you standing in that doorway while I played." He glanced at the wedding ring on her gloved finger. "Is Lord Manvers a loving husband, my lady? Does he possess your heart as well as your hand?"

"My husband is dead," she whispered, suddenly unable to bear being so close to him anymore. Gathering her skirts, she turned and walked away, her train rustling through the scattered sand on the floor and the many black beads on her shawl sparkling beneath the chandeliers.

She retreated hastily from the ballroom, conscious of how much he had unsettled her. A great number of people watched her flight and there was a ripple of murmurs as the speculative whispers began. Was history about to repeat itself? Was the Earl of Wallborough's elder daughter about to submit to the embrace of a man who was the very image of her dead husband?

Her cheeks hot, she hurried up the steps and reached the relative safety of the vestibule, but it was outside she wished to be, outside in the cool night air where she could compose herself, unseen by anyone. She remembered the library then, for it had French windows opening onto the terrace and the gardens, and without hesitation she hurried toward it now.

The rear of the house was quiet, well away from the ballroom, and it was with relief that she opened the gold-and-white door and stepped into the moonlit room beyond. The silver light streaming in through the tall windows lay in pale shafts over the rich crimsons and purples of the Persian carpet, and the hundreds of volumes on the shelves lining the walls muffled all sound as she crossed to the windows, but as her fingers closed over the handle, a voice startled her, making her whirl about to search the shadows.

"Good evening, Alabeth." Piers Castleton lounged in one of the chairs watching her, his cravat undone and his long legs stretched out before him. His glance swept slowly over her, coming to rest on her face as she stood in the full moonlight, the rubies glowing against her white throat.

He smiled at her silence. "How sad it is that so intelligent a woman should allow something as imaginary and inconsequential as a ghost to cloud her otherwise excellent judgment."

Refusing to be drawn and determined to avoid speaking to him, she turned back to the window and tried to open it.

"The window is locked—that, at least, is not imaginary," he said, getting to his feet. "Although in your present frame of mind you no doubt believe the key is there simply because there is a lock—just as you believe that Robert's memory is sweet simply because he had a charming smile."

"I don't wish to speak to you, sir," she said icily, "least of all about Robert."

"Really? How strange, for I could have sworn that it was because of Robert that you are trying to flee out into the night."

She flushed. "It is none of your concern why I do anything."

"I have chosen to make it my concern—for the moment, at least. Believe me, I do have your best interest at heart, although you are determined to believe to the contrary."

Pressing her lips angrily together, she said nothing more, hurrying back across the room to leave. His voice halted her. "The handsome, winning ghost you trod a measure with a moment since was no ghost; it was very much a flesh-and-blood Polish aristocrat with your seduction on his mind. Imagine what you will about Robert, Alabeth, but be under no illusion about Zaleski, for it could prove your undoing. He is no laggard in the pursuit of the fair sex, his reputation in that direction has more than preceded him, and the brief contact you've already had with him should be proof enough that I do not speak lightly."

"Are you presuming to offer me advice?" she demanded, her voice quivering.

"Yes, I rather believe I am."

"Well, spare yourself, for your advice is neither sought nor welcome."

"Nonetheless, you appear to be in need of it, madam."

"How dare you—"

"You are at risk, Alabeth, because you have made yourself vulnerable to Robert's memory. Be sensible. Zaleski is
no figment of your imagination, and he is certainly not the
reincarnation of the somewhat rosy notion you have of
your late lord."

"You speak of illusions, sirrah, so let me tell you that I
am under none where you are concerned, for you are
everything that is odious and treacherous."

"Believe what you will," he said, turning away, "for I
have said my piece. Perhaps I should have spared myself
the trouble of being concerned about you after all."

"Being *concerned* about me . . . ?" Her fury at this
presumption threatened to get the better of her, but with a
great effort she overcame the urge to go to him and strike
him. Instead, she turned on her heel and walked from the
room, leaving the door open behind her so that he could
hear her light, angry steps on the marble floor.

As she hurried away, however, her anger became even
more bitter, for while he had been so kindly offering her
advice on her conduct, she had not once had the wit to
point out his indiscretions with Jillian. Once again she had
allowed him to get the better of her, and she had left him
with the last word.

11

Jillian had not taken at all kindly to Alabeth's strictures concerning her conduct at the ball, nor had she been pleased at not being able to even meet the Count, whereas Alabeth had been sought out by him and had not used the opportunity to mention her sister's great desire to be his pupil. The uneasy truce which had existed between the Earl of Wallborough's daughters faded away, with Jillian flouncing to her room on their return from Seaham House, announcing that she would not be accompanying Alabeth either to the private viewing at the Royal Academy or to the British Museum.

Alabeth had retired to her own bed feeling very ragged, and her fitful sleep had been disturbed by dreams in which she danced with the Count again—or was it with Robert? And was it Piers Castleton's indistinct figure she could see in the shadows? All in all, she awoke the following morning with a headache and feeling as exhausted as if she had not slept at all. She was certainly not in the mood to inspect the paintings at the Royal Academy, or to show any great enthusiasm about the contents of the British Museum, and her mood became positively sour when she was greeted with the news that Jillian was standing by her attitude of the previous night and was remaining in her room, pleading a purely invented headache.

Taking her breakfast alone in the morning room, Alabeth glanced at some fragments of torn card in the hearth, and when she went to retrieve them, she knew that Jillian's headache had not prevented her from coming down early to deliberately choose this particular invitation

as proof of her defiance. The invitation was to a select
dinner party thrown by Lady Dexter, and Jillian's sole
reason for tearing it up was that Charles Allister was to be
the only other unattached guest and would most certainly
have been paired off with Jillian, to whom the invitation
had been addressed. Lady Dexter was Charles' kinswoman
and had obviously been approached by him, with the intention of being placed next to Jillian, but that young lady
had no intention whatsoever of giving even an inch in her
attitude toward him—hence the furiously torn pieces of
gold-edged card scattered in the hearth.

Alabeth pursed her lips crossly. Jillian was being
odiously difficult, but there was little to gain for the
moment in remonstrating with her as she was in too much
of a pet. Perhaps it would be much wiser to let her fume in
her room all day with just her own bad company; maybe
that would prove a salutary experience and be a sovereign
remedy for this latest fit of the tantrums. With a deep
breath, Alabeth went to prepare to go out.

Wearing an unbuttoned red spencer over a white muslin
gown, she set off a little later to meet Octavia at the Royal
Academy. On her head she wore a little hat with an
upturned brim and a jaunty plume, and her pagoda
parasol twirled busily behind her, for she was determined
to put Jillian's spoiled behavior from her thoughts. She
was equally determined not to think at all about Piers
Castleton, or the Count, or anything else which might dis-
turb her equilibrium.

The Royal Academy was uninteresting. Try as she
would, she could not enthuse about the array of paintings
suspended from every conceivable inch of the walls, and
she knew that she was not being exactly sparkling company
for Octavia. The much-vaunted visit to the British
Museum, housed at Montague House in Great Russell
Street, was hardly less inspiring, in spite of the undoubted
cock of the snook the presence of ladies gave to those

hallowed rooms. They were led through chambers filled with stuffed birds and animals, many of which, to Alabeth's rather jaundiced eye, appeared to be in an advanced state of decay, and through more rooms containing the arms, dress, and ornaments of savages, a collection of minerals, antiquities from Herculaneum and Pompeii, and even more from Egypt. There was a curious slab of dark porphyry from Rosetta, marked out in three languages, including the hieroglyphics of ancient Egypt, which did interest her a great deal, but apart from that she found the whole visit decidedly flat.

Octavia took exquisite delight in exacting full revenge for the fact that ladies were excluded, thus almost certainly ensuring that the exclusion continued for some considerable time to come, if the affronted expressions of the various gentlemen who overheard her pointed remarks were anything to go by. Normally Alabeth would have entered more into the spirit of things, but today somehow she just could not; her mood was too low and she did not seem to have the resilience to shrug it off. Perhaps it was having to contend with Jillian, or maybe it was the unsettling effect of having met the Count the previous evening. It could even have been the result of having had yet another disagreeable meeting with Piers Castleton, who had the uncanny knack of completely destroying her poise. Whatever it was, it made her poor company, and Octavia was not altogether displeased when the time came to depart.

Alabeth felt a little guilty for having undoubtedly been a damper on the proceedings, and as the landau set off along Oxford Street on its way back to Berkeley Square, she suddenly decided that perhaps it would be better if she took a drive in Hyde Park first, as the fresh air would probably do her a great deal of good and might put her in a better frame of mind to deal with Jillian.

Hyde Park, as usual, was crowded, but she was indeed

beginning to feel a little better as the landau passed
beneath the dappled shade of the trees and the slight breeze
played with the fringe of her parasol. A moment later,
however, the lighter mood was shattered when she happened to glance across the grass and saw Jillian riding
alone with Piers Castleton.

Alabeth could not believe her eyes, for it was very bad
form of Jillian to plead indisposition in order to escape
previous engagements, and then to be so foolish as to
display the truth to the whole of fashionable society by
riding in so public a place as Hyde Park. And to make
matters worse, she was behaving with a great deal of
intimacy toward Piers, leaning toward him, smiling up into
his eyes, and even being so bold as to reach across and
momentarily rest her hand on his. Even as Alabeth stared
in unbelieving dismay, the two horses were reined in and
Piers dismounted. Jillian seemed to be pointing down to
one of the leathers of her sidesaddle, and Alabeth was
appalled to see how she flicked her riding habit aside to
afford him an excellent view of her neat little ankles. And
all under the guise of pretending the leather needed attention.

Alabeth was speechless, quite unable to credit that
anyone, even Jillian, could be that indiscreet. Even Lady
Adelina Carver would have shrunk from quite such an ex-
hibition, and to do Piers a little justice, he was obviously a
little taken aback and seemed reluctant to comply with
Jillian's request. All eyes were surely riveted on the curious
little scene, thought Alabeth, feeling almost haunted at the
awful apparition of her sister's tattered character being
merrily savaged by every tongue in every drawing room
across London. It was the final straw; Alabeth could
brook no more nonsense from Jillian, and as the landau
carried her inexorably on her way across the park, she
determined that the time had come for a final confrontation—one from which Lady Jillian Carstairs would not

recover in a hurry. And as for Piers Castleton . . . Well, maybe the time had come for the error of *his* ways to be pointed out to him. He was so free with his advice and comments, so sure that he was without fault, that it would undoubtedly come as a great shock to find that there was someone who could justifiably criticize *him*.

Bristling with anger, she ordered the coachman to return to Berkeley Square, and her fury bubbled still more when she was told by Sanderson that Lady Jillian had gone to visit Mrs. Haverstock, an old friend of the family who had just arrived in Town. Mrs. Haverstock, indeed! The minx had deliberately fibbed in order to steal out and keep an assignation with a rogue who should have known a great deal better.

Her fingers drummed impatiently on the arm of her chair as she sat waiting in the drawing room for Jillian to return. An hour passed before she heard the hooves clattering outside, and she rose to see Jillian dismounting and handing the reins to the waiting groom. Holding her cumbersome riding skirt, she hurried into the house, to be told by Sanderson that Lady Alabeth awaited her in the drawing room.

With an air of complete innocence, not untinged with a certain gleam of triumph, Jillian entered the drawing room, removing her gloves and placing them on a table, together with her riding crop. Her smile was cool, her mien haughty. "You wish to see me?"

"I trust you found Mrs. Haverstock in excellent health?"

"Oh, yes. She vowed she was delighted to see me as simply everyone appeared to have gone to the Royal Academy. I stayed with her for a considerable time."

"Indeed? You've come straight from her house, have you?"

"Yes."

"Then you must have passed her in the doorway, for she

was at the Royal Academy and asked especially after you.''

Jillian went pale. "There is some mistake—"

"Yes, missy, and you've made it. I know *precisely* what you were doing this morning and it certainly was not calling upon Mrs. Haverstock. I saw you in Hyde Park with Piers Castleton, as I suspect everyone else did too, and I was appalled at your immodest and forward conduct.''

Jillian was now visibly shaken. "I suppose you were spying on me again," she cried.

"I was not doing any such thing."

"Hyde Park does not lie between this house and Great Russell Street.''

"I decided to go for a drive, and it is just as well that I did, Jillian, for otherwise I would not have seen your incredible folly. How *could* you behave like that? How could you? Are you so contemptuous of your reputation?''

"I only rode with him," Jillian said defensively, turning away then to bite her lip and try to hide how upset she was becoming.

"Propriety demands more demureness than you seem capable of, Jillian; you behaved more like a Cyprian than a proper young lady. What would Father have thought had he witnessed your behavior? Well? You are impossible, and you are making my task impossible too, for how can I be expected to present you to society as a desirable bride and excellent match when you lie and scheme to prove the very opposite? Today you broke many rules, not least of which was that if you are going to break a prior appointment, you do not then do all in your power to be seen and thus risk having your deceit reported. You agreed to conduct yourself with more decorum. Well, if this is a sample of your notion of decorum, then it is obvious that I dare not let you leave this house. I shall inform Sanderson of my decision.''

Jillian was aghast. "You would humiliate me in front of the servants?"

"I know of no other way, Jillian, for you have shown yourself capable of lying in order to have your own way."

"You cannot imprison me. I won't permit it."

"There is nothing you can do to stop me, for Father left me in sole charge of you—and that means in charge of your good name and character, two items for which you appear to have scant respect. And don't think to resurrect my past escapades, for it will avail you of nothing. I may have played with fire, but I was singularly fortunate in not being burned. I am aware of my sins, Jillian, which makes me doubly aware of yours. And if you stop to consider for a moment, that is precisely why Father wanted me to look after you, isn't it?"

Jillian said nothing, but she looked very rebellious; two specks of red stained her cheekbones and her blue eyes were bright indeed with unshed tears.

Alabeth's mind was totally made up now. "I shall inform Sanderson that you are to be confined to the house until further notice, and I shall nip this undesirable affair with Piers Castleton in the bud by paying that gentleman a visit."

Jillian was suddenly quite ashen. "You cannot mean that—"

"I do mean it, for I simply cannot have any further misconduct like this, and he will have to be told. I don't know what madness has got into you, Jillian, but I shall do my utmost to combat it, that much I promise you."

"Don't go to him," begged Jillian, tears shimmering on her lashes. "Please don't—"

"I have to; you've left me with no alternative." But Alabeth was a little taken aback by the obvious horror with which this statement was received.

"I've done nothing," whispered Jillian, "nothing at all—"

"You know that that is not the case. I trusted you,
Jillian, and you deliberately broke faith. I should have
known from that moment we encountered Piers and
Charles in Hyde Park that there was a great deal more to
your 'acquaintance' with him than met the eye."

Jillian's breath caught on a gasp, her lips moved as if she
wanted to say something, and then she turned on her heel,
running from the drawing room and up the stairs toward
her own room. Alabeth heard the door slam and then there
was silence. She was trembling a little herself as she took a
long breath to steady her nerves. She would have to be true
to her word; she would have to go face Piers and tell him
that she expected him to stay away from Jillian from now
on. It was her duty as Jillian's guardian to do that, but it
would not be an easy task, not an easy one at all. . . .

12

The footman stood aside and Alabeth stepped into the vestibule of Piers Castleton's elegant house in Cavendish Street. The walls were a pristine white and hung with oriental tapestries, the floor was of pink marble, and the only pieces of furniture were two Indian sofas set in recesses on either side of the fireplace. An elliptical staircase rose from the far end of the vestibule, vanishing between immense columns which stretched up to the domed roof far above.

"I will inform Sir Piers that you have called, my lady." The footman bowed and left her.

She watched him mount the staircase. She felt a little less sure of herself now that she was here, but she was determined that she would put an end to Jillian's liaison, however much it took.

It seemed that she stood there waiting for an unconscionable length of time, but then at last the footman returned. "If you will come this way, my lady, Sir Piers will receive you in the green saloon."

Her heart was thundering as she followed him up the staircase and along the wide passage to the pale green-and-gold doors. He thrust the doors open and announced her.

The green saloon was done up in the style of ancient Rome, the chairs and sofa looking very much as if they had been plucked from a villa in that city. The wallpaper was striped in shades of green, the woodwork was painted white, and the design on the octagonal carpet echoed the beige, pink, and green of the elaborately decorated ceiling. At the tall windows there were gold satin curtains with green cords and tassels, and the breeze which crept into the room moved the crystal droplets of the chandelier above the circular mahogany table.

Piers stood by the huge mantelpiece, one boot resting on the gleaming fender. He wore a dark-brown coat and fawn breeches, and his full and complicated cravat spilled over his maroon waistcoat. He waited until the footman had closed the doors again. "Good afternoon, Alabeth, and to what do I owe this unexpected honor?"

"I think you know full well, sir."

"Do I, indeed? I can see from your icy demeanor that this is not a pleasant social call."

"Your conduct is quite unforgivable, sir, and I have come to demand that you desist immediately."

He straightened. "What conduct?"

"Your pursuit of my sister."

"I am not pursuing her."

"Last night you danced three times with her and encouraged her most lamentably, and this morning you rode alone with her in Hyde Park, after she had broken previous engagements by pleading illness, and you conducted yourself in a way which must have been obvious to all and sundry."

"I say again that I am not pursuing her," he said, maintaining a level tone, although with some difficulty, "and while I admit that I may have been a little remiss—"

"*Remiss?*" She was amazed. "Is that all you can say?"

"What else? I should have done more to discourage her, and in that, and that alone, I have been at fault."

"You have pursued my sister, sir, and your conduct is certainly more serious than the word 'remiss' would seem to suggest. I don't profess to know what has gone on between you since you met at Chatsworth last year, but—"

"Nothing has gone on," he interrupted angrily. "And I'm damned if I'm going to stand here and let you accuse me of all manner of things of which I am innocent. Until that first time I met you and your sister in Hyde Park, when I was with Charles Allister, I had only met Lady Jillian once before—at Chatsworth, when I danced once with her. I have since met her at Octavia Seaham's ball and again today, when I happened to encounter her in Hyde Park when she was out riding. If that amounts to pursuing her, then I am guilty."

"Last night you danced an inexcusable three times with her and thus allowed her to make a mistake from which you, sir, could easily have saved her. You know full well that it is frowned upon for a young lady, especially at her first London ball, to be seen too much in the company of any one man. You chose to ignore that. Furthermore, you arranged an assignation with her this morning in Hyde Park, at which assignation she behaved with a familiarity which you did nothing to discourage. You are contemptible, sir, for you've casually and thoughtlessly allowed her to compromise her reputation. I find that despicable."

A nerve flickered at his temple, the only sign of his own carefully controlled anger. "You seem to imagine, madam, that it is always in the power of the gentleman to guide the situation. Let me tell you that it is not, especially with a young lady as impetuous as your sister. She asked me—no, begged me—to dance again with her, and really, although I knew it was inadvisable, she was not prepared to be fobbed off with any lame excuse. I did *not* arrange to meet her in Hyde Park; she knew I was going to be there, having overheard me mention it, and she made certain that she came across me. We rode together for a while—"

"In a most intimate manner."

"Dear God, woman, I find you exasperating at times," he cried, "for I am attempting to explain what happened and you are interrupting. I rode with your sister for a while, and then she told me that she feared the girth of her saddle was a little loose and she was in danger of falling. What would you have me do, Alabeth? Ignore her and then leave her to fall? Instead, I decided it would be wiser to see if indeed the girth was loose, and that is what I did, although I confess that I did not suspect for one moment that she was going to reveal her ankles both to me and to the rest of the world. I expected her to dismount—she did not. I say again that I have been a little remiss, for I knew that she was forming some sort of attachment for me and I did not do enough to discourage her, but then neither did I *en*courage her.''

"You should have behaved more like a gentleman and less like a seducer of innocence,'' she retorted.

His eyes flashed. "A seducer of innocence? By all that's holy, you begin to go too far—''

"I will go as far as is necessary to keep you away from my sister.''

"Will you, by God? I wonder how far that is?''

"I trust that it will not be necessary to find out.''

His eyes were half-closed, resting almost speculatively on her pale, angry face. "Are you always this challenging, Alabeth?''

She ignored him. "Will you refrain from any contact with my sister?''

"Yes.''

She stared at him. "You will?''

"Quite willingly. You see, although she is delightfully pretty and engaging, she is too young and indisciplined for me. I prefer my women to be a little more discreet and to behave with more maturity.''

"I do not care how you prefer your women, sir, merely that your preference does not include Jillian.'' Satisfied that she had achieved her aim, she turned to leave him.

He took two strides which brought him to her before she realized what was happening, and she could only gasp as his arm went around her waist and she was turned to face him, his fingers cupping her chin and his lips only inches from her. "Oh, my preference certainly does not include your sister," he murmured, smiling a little, "but you, my dearest Alabeth, you are very much to my taste."

He bent to kiss her, his lips moving slowly over hers as he drew her even closer. She was too startled to move as his skillful lips teased her, rendering her incapable of thinking clearly and robbing her of any will to begin resisting. His kiss stirred forgotten senses, caused her blood to flow more warmly through her veins, and made every nerve seem alive only to him. For the headiest and most unbelievable of moments, she was on the brink of responding, wanting to cling to him, but then sanity returned and furiously she began to thrust away from him.

He gave a short laugh, releasing her and smiling scornfully into her angry eyes. "Perhaps that will teach you, madam, not to come here wagging your finger at me and accusing me of evil intentions toward your sister. I'm tired of you, Lady Alabeth Manvers, tired of your constant dislike and tired of being held to blame for everything that has gone wrong in your life. I am no more guilty of attempting to seduce your sister than I was of luring Robert from the paths of righteousness. I assure you, madam, that he fell by the wayside all by himself. This is positively your last chance, Alabeth, for I swear that if you provoke me once more, then I shall tell you some home truths which are long overdue and which only honor has prevented me from saying before."

Mortified and humiliated, she stared at him for a moment, her pride bruised and her composure wrecked. Then, catching her skirts, she ran from the room, but as she descended the staircase, it was as if he held her still, kissed her still . . .

She didn't look back as the landau conveyed her away, but her cheeks were damp with tears. "I shall tell you some home truths which are long overdue and which only honor has prevented me from saying before." She stared out at the passing Mayfair houses, and they seemed to melt away,

and suddenly it was a warm August afternoon at Charterleigh again and Robert was presenting her to Piers for the
first time. The glance of his gray eyes was so disturbing,
for it was as if he could see right into her soul, and
the touch of his hand was like a sudden awakening, a
shock which breathed more excitement into her life than
she had ever known before. But Robert had died, and she
believed Piers to have been responsible—how, then, could
it be anything but wicked to be so drawn to him? She
closed her eyes, her head bowed.

13

The landau entered Berkeley Square and to her horror she saw a rather travel-stained chaise drawing up outside the house; she recognized it immediately as belonging to the Wallborough steward, Mr. Bateman. Hastily she dabbed her eyes with her handkerchief, trying to compose herself and trusting that the marks of her weeping were not too evident. Oh, how she hated this day, already so long and wearisome, and now quite obviously not finished with yet. The landau came alongside the curb and halted, and taking a deep breath, her head held high, she alighted and entered the house.

The steward had been shown into the drawing room, and he rose immediately to his feet as she came in. "Good afternoon, Lady Alabeth."

"Good afternoon, Mr. Bateman."

"I trust that you received my brief communication."

"I did indeed, sir," she replied, sitting down and gesturing that he should do the same.

He settled himself slowly in a well-remembered way which took her back to her childhood, when it had been a fine adventure to visit him and take Shrewsbury cakes and a glass of perry—something of which her father would not have approved, had he known. The steward still appeared to wear the same gray-powdered wig and even the same ribbon, and he looked as comfortable and comforting as ever as he smiled at her, his glance lingering very briefly on her tear-marked eyes. "And how are you, Lady Alabeth?"

"I'm very well and I trust that I find you the same."

He nodded. "Perhaps I find it a little more difficult to

rise from my bed these days, but apart from that, I go along in the same, time-honored way. But enough of these pleasantries, for I have no doubt that you wish to learn what I can tell you about Lady Jillian.''

"There is something, then.''

"Oh, yes, I fear that there is. You must understand, my lady, that in speaking to you I am breaking a confidence, for the Earl wished above all else to hush the whole matter up.''

Her heart was sinking still further. ''Whatever you tell me will not go further, sir.''

"I know that. Well, it happened last year, when Lady Jillian accompanied the Earl to an autumn ball at Chatsworth. She met Sir Piers Castleton, who is, I fully realize, the gentleman to whom you were referring in your letter. I fear that Lady Jillian formed an attachment for him, an attachment which was in some measure returned, for she was being indiscreet enough to exchange letters of a certain intimacy with him. I hasten to add that there was nothing in the affair to suggest that she had—er—succumbed completely.'' He looked a little embarrassed, clearing his throat and shifting his position just a little. ''Indeed, nothing would have been known of it all had not the Earl happened upon one of the letters she had written, and on reading it realized that she was in the habit of going out to keep secret assignations with Sir Piers in Wallborough Woods.''

"Oh, no!'' Alabeth could see Piers' angry face again as he denied pursuing Jillian. Liar! Despicable liar!

"How they managed to carry on such a liaison without anyone realizing defies comprehension,'' went on the agent, ''but they did, and it would probably have continued, had not the incriminating letter been found.''

Piers' voice rang in Alabeth's ears. ''Until that first time I met you and your sister in Hyde Park, when I was with Charles Allister, I had only met Lady Jillian once before—

at Chatsworth, when I danced once with her. I have since met her at Octavia Seaham's ball and again today, when I happened to encounter her in Hyde Park when she was out riding.'' Oh, how infamous he was, how shamelessly he had lied, swearing his innocence when all the time he was so very guilty.

Mr. Bateman was silent for a moment. "The Earl was naturally very anxious, for Sir Piers was not really very suitable, having been involved in that duel in which the Russian died, and so when he heard that Sir Piers was going to Europe this summer, he decided that Lady Jillian *must* be brought out during her lover's absence, the hope being that she might make a match and thus be prevented from perhaps ruining her reputation. Then came the Earl's appointment to the post in Madras, a post which he knew he must accept but which would also interfere with the supervision of Lady Jillian's Season. At first it was intended that Lady Silchester should have charge of everything, but then her health broke down.''

"Hence his visit to me."

"Yes, my lady."

"I should have been told all this. It was wrong of my father to keep it from me."

"I agree, my lady, and indeed I advised him to tell you, but he felt that it would be better to let it all die down. With Sir Piers being out of the country—"

"He is not out of the country; he is very much here in Town and indeed I spoke with him not half an hour ago."

The steward stared at her. "Oh, dear!"

"Quite. I find it quite unforgivable of my father to expect me to take on such a responsibility and yet to conceal important information which has a great bearing on the whole thing.''

"He had two reasons for not wishing to tell you, my lady, and to him they were excellent reasons. To begin with, he knew that you and Lady Jillian had already fallen

out because of the regrettable affair with Captain Francis
earlier last year, and he had no wish to further antagonize
the differences because of this new development, especially
as the gentleman concerned was Sir Piers Castleton. And
second, he didn't wish to tell you of his anxieties, for he
feared that you might feel it reflected on you and all that
happened in the past when you met Lord Manvers. He
spent a long evening with me before finally deciding what
to do, my lady, and believe me, he honestly felt that
this course was the best one—for both you and Lady Jillian."

Slowly she got to her feet, crossing to the window and
looking out over the square. Well, at last she knew the
truth, after having been lied to on all sides. She stared at
the gently moving plane trees. "Nothing has gone on. And
I'm damned if I'm going to stand here and let you accuse
me of all manner of things of which I am innocent."

The steward got to his feet. "I have told you all I know,
Lady Alabeth, and I beg you to remember that I have
broken my word to the Earl."

She managed a smile. "I promised you that I would be
discreet, that I would do nothing to jeopardize your position, and I stand by that promise. I am only too grateful
that you trusted me enough to tell me, and you may rest
assured that what has passed between us tonight will go no
further. I just had to know the truth, for it was impossible
to know if I was doing the right thing all the time when I
was constantly aware that there were matters I had not
been told."

"I quite understand that, my lady. I am afraid that Lady
Jillian is—well, rather too romantically inclined. She seeks
true love and mistakenly believes she has found it in every
handsome gentleman who pays court to her."

Alabeth gave a small laugh. "I wish, Mr. Bateman, that
she would indeed find that true love, for then we would all
have some peace."

He smiled fondly at her. "It will all come out right in the end."

"You always were an incurable optimist, sir."

"A steward must be, if he is to survive, my lady."

"Yes, I suppose you are right."

"Well, I must go now."

"You will not take some refreshment? And surely you intend to stay overnight?"

"I have taken a room at a hostelry named the White Hart, my lady."

She smiled then. "Which no doubt has the most iniquitous cockpit in London."

"It does indeed, my lady."

"And you've brought some of those odious birds with you from Wallborough?"

"I've a mind to show these Londoners how a good Derbyshire bird can lick them."

"I wish you well, but warn you that the gentlemen of the White Hart know a thing or two."

He rubbed the side of his nose with his finger and winked. "So do I, my lady, so do I."

When he had gone, she sat down again, thinking things over—and in particular thinking about how monstrously Piers had behaved throughout. How *could* he have faced her so blatantly, denying everything and even having the gall to claim that *she* had been making baseless accusations! Baseless? Why, each one was now proved beyond a doubt to be well founded, each one was now proved beyond a doubt to be well founded, each one more than justified, and yet he had heaped scorned upon her, humiliated her . . . And then there was Jillian herself, denied so casually by her noble lover . . . What was to become of her?

At that moment the drawing room door was opened very slowly and Jillian's tearstained face peeped apprehensively in.

Alabeth straightened. "Hello, Jillian."

Jillian came in and closed the door. She was very pale and nervous, twisting her handkerchief over and over again and looking thoroughly wretched. "H-have you seen him?"

"I have."

The large blue eyes filled with fresh tears. "Oh."

"Jillian . . ."

"You know all about the letter, don't you? That's why you went to see Piers today, because you already knew and feared things were still going on."

Alabeth was relieved that Jillian had confessed this much, and she saw no point at all in revealing that the letter's existence had been discovered *after* the visit to Piers. "I did not mention the letter to him, Jillian, and he denied absolutely everything anyway."

Jillian stared at her, her eyes suddenly and surprisingly much brighter. "You *didn't* mention the letter?"

"No."

"Oh, I'm so glad!" Jillian sat down and it seemed to Alabeth that she did not know whether to laugh or cry. The tears in her eyes were certainly different now. "Alabeth, you'll never know how relieved I am."

Alabeth was puzzled, for what difference did mentioning the letter make to it all? Letter or no letter, Piers had flatly denied any involvement with Jillian, he had showed a lamentable lack of consideration or gallantry, and yet Jillian professed herself to be glad. It did not make sense, for surely bitter tears were more to be expected under the circumstances. . . .

Jilliam seemed, in fact, as if a great weight had been lifted from her shoulders. She even managed a smile. "I'm not a-a fallen woman, you know."

"Jillian!"

"Well, you know what I mean. I'm still as perfect as any

gentleman would expect of a prospective bride." She bit her lip then. "I don't want you to think I—"

"I don't think anything like that, you know that I don't," interrupted Alabeth gently.

"I'm so sorry for being so very bad to you. Even as I did it, I knew I was in the wrong, and I promise right here and now that I shall be a different person from now on."

Now Alabeth was thoroughly perplexed, for Jillian's reaction simply did not add up to the facts. "Jillian, are you sure you're feeling quite well?"

"I'm feeling very well indeed, truly I am, and I just want to forget how odious I've been. I've learned my lesson now, truly I have, and you won't have any more trouble from me. I'll even write to accept the invitation to dine at Lady Dexter's. There, is that not proof of my good intentions?"

Alabeth could not think of anything to say, for this complete reversal was quite bewildering.

Jillian smiled again, reaching over to take her hand. "I don't know why I've been so horrible recently, I didn't really mean any of it. In my heart I knew you only acted out of love for me when you went to Father about that dreadful Captain Francis, but I simply couldn't bring myself to admit it. I think that's a great deal of my trouble. I can never bring myself to admit it when I'm in the wrong. Anyway, I know that I behaved badly then, and I've been behaving badly ever since. It won't happen again."

"And what about your feelings for Piers?"

"I don't think I really ever had any." Jillian smiled, a little shamefaced. "He was just there, he came along so soon after Captain Francis— He is in the past as far as I'm concerned, and you really must believe that, for it is the truth."

Alabeth knew that indeed it was, that Piers had ceased to exist for Jillian, who was indeed contrite and meant to turn over a new leaf. But why this sudden change? Just because the letter had not been mentioned? No matter how Alabeth approached the problem, Jillian's reaction simply did not add up. But then, was it really important what reason lay behind it? All that mattered was that the awkwardness and unpleasantness was over and things looked set to be agreeable again between the Earl of Wallborough's daughters.

Jillian went to take the "accepted" invitations down from the mantelpiece, sifting through them with more interest than she had ever shown hitherto.

"Oh, Alabeth, I'm so looking forward to the fete at Carlton House, for I shall see at last if the Prince of Wales is as handsome as they say."

"He's certainly as plump as they say."

"And then there's Ascot week at Stoneleigh Park, and the water party there before that." Jillian looked ashamed then as she glanced at Alabeth. "I've been atrocious, haven't I?"

"In a word, yes."

"I shall be very good from now on, you'll be proud of me, you'll see. I shall absolutely dazzle Charles Allister at Lady Dexter's."

"I feel quite sorry for him."

"Why do you say that?"

"Because the poor fellow was at your feet when you were being disagreeable; he'll be positively devastated if you begin to be agreeable instead."

"I know that Father wishes me to marry him."

"But you do not find him to your liking."

"Oh, I *like* him, it's just that—well, he's so very dull. He isn't exciting at all; he's just nice and gentle, he says nothing to provoke me at all, and I feel that I could scream sometimes, truly I do."

"Please contain that urge at all costs."

"I will." Jillian gave a rueful smile. "I won't let rip at Carlton House, if that's what you fear."

"You do, and I'll personally extinguish you."

They smiled at each other then and suddenly Jillian ran to her sister, kneeling beside her chair and flinging her arms around her. "Please forgive me, Alabeth."

Alabeth kissed the soft curly hair. "I forgive you, you wretch."

Jillian sat back on her heels. "And what about you and the Count?"

"What do you mean?"

"Will you take it further with him?"

"Jillian!"

"Oh, come on now, Alabeth—"

"I have no intention of taking anything further with anyone."

"He is remarkably like Robert, everyone was commenting upon it."

Alabeth looked away. "It makes no difference."

"Doesn't it? I thought he would eat you, and I didn't think you were exactly shrinking away from him."

"You have too much to say for yourself."

"But isn't it the very height of romance? You were swept off your feet by Robert; you were passionately in love with each other and he made you his bride. Now he's gone from you, but instead the Count steps into your life. Oh, Alabeth, I think it truly the most romantic coincidence, and I know that if a man like the Count looked at me the way he looks at you—well, I'd most certainly take it further; in fact, I'd take it to the ends of the earth."

"Jillian Carstairs, you are incorrigible, do you know that? I've never known anyone so totally immersed in a search for romance. You see it at every corner."

"And I'll truly find it one day, you see if I don't. I've made mistakes so far, but there won't by any more."

"I sincerely hope not."

"I still think you should encourage the Count. Octavia says you should, because it would do you good."

"Octavia would."

"And if you did, you'd be able to put in a word for me, tell him that I'm just the very one to be his first pupil—" She ducked as Alabeth threw a cushion at her.

14

It was well known that the Prince of Wales' fete at Carlton House for important figures in the world of French art was much frowned upon at Court. Indeed, anything connected with France was frowned upon, the King and Queen finding it justifiably impossible to forget that the French had beheaded their own Royal Family. However, the Prince was torn between his own repugnance at what had been done in Paris and his desire at all costs to thumb his nose at his father. Being an important and genuine patron of the arts, and a sincere admirer of the Whigs and Charles Fox, who admired anything to do with the revolution, he had decided upon his fete as being the perfect vehicle for his purpose. The *beau monde* found itself able to accept the invitations, for whatever one thought of the French, art was always art and must be encouraged.

The invitations stipulated an arrival time of nine in the evening, but already by eight there was a solid block of carriages and chairs reaching from Carlton House to the top of St. James's. By nine the Wallborough landau was part of a crush which extended to Bond Street, and Alabeth and Jillian were resigned to a long delay.

It was a splendid evening, warm and sunny, with a hint of approaching coolness after an almost thundery heat all day, but Jillian was hardly aware of the weather, she was too excited about seeing the Prince for the first time and inspecting the magnificence of Carlton House, which was said by many to be one of the most superb mansions in the whole of Europe.

She looked very lovely, with tiny strings of pearls in her

golden hair and a jeweled comb which flashed in the
evening sunlight. Her gown was of particularly delicate
white lawn, its dainty bodice stitched with more little
pearls, and her shawl was embroidered with beautiful
sprays of pink roses. She looked every inch a young lady of
quality and had begun to really enjoy the Season, being
very much the center of male attention wherever she went.

She had been true to her promise on the afternoon of
Alabeth's confrontation with Piers, and was now her old
self, being sweet, charming, and very agreeable company
indeed, as the large numbers of admirers at Almack's had
been certain evidence. Almack's had disappointed her,
however, for although Octavia's acquisition of the coveted
voucher had been greeted with squeaks of excitement and
she had set off in the Seaham carriage that Wednesday
evening in a high state of anticipation bordering on the
ecstatic, she had returned in a very different frame of
mind. The temple of high fashion had taken a considerable
tumble in her estimation and she stated quite bluntly that
she could not imagine why everyone wished to be seen
there. The proceedings had been very dull, the orchestra
uninspiring; there had been no iced champagne to liven
things up, only lemonade and stewed tea, and the food
consisted of bread and butter and stale cake. Yes, indeed,
Almack's had definitely failed to live up to its reputation,
and Alabeth had had to point out at some length that being
on its list was very important and necessary to a young
lady, and that she would therefore have to put up with
bread and lemonade. Jillian had grumbled a little, but had
consoled herself with the fact that at least the place had
been filled to capacity with eligible young men, nearly all
of them flatteringly attentive. Her *faux pas* at Octavia's
ball and in Hyde Park seemed to have been forgotten, her
more recent appearances in society having been much more
decorous and acceptable, and all in all, she was approved
of. There seemed no hint of regret about the ending of her

affair with Piers Castleton; it was almost as if it had never been, and now she was set upon enjoying the Season to the full. Her eyes shone as she sat impatiently on the edge of the landau's velvet seat, and Alabeth would not have been at all surprised if she had suggested they got out and walked, which would not have done at all!

Alabeth did not display any of Jillian's excitement or impatience, for she had been to Carlton House a number of times, both before her marriage and then as Robert's wife, for Robert had been a great favorite with the Prince. She looked cool and composed as she sat opposite her sister, her gossamer light muslin gown looking very white indeed in the fading sunlight. It was a plain gown, unadorned in any way, but she more than made up for it with the jaunty crimson plumes in her jeweled hair and her favorite ruby necklace at her throat. Her shawl was a dazzling affair, embroidered all over with golden threads, as was her reticule, and she looked very elegant and poised, as if nothing in the world could ruffle her. But inwardly she was not so calm and assured; in fact, she was more than a little apprehensive. Tonight she would undoubtedly see Piers Castleton again, for the first time since he had humiliated her with his scornful kiss, and she was not looking forward at all to the encounter, for she felt more shamed than ever when she remembered how very close she had come to responding to him.

Tonight, too, she would see Count Adam Zaleski again, for he was to play for the French guests of honor. She had thought a great deal about the Count, knowing full well that he intended to pursue her, but how would she react? She knew that she found him attractive, but then there could be very few women who would not have been unsettled by such a man. When he played the pianoforte, he could make love with his music; his looks had been justifiably described as divine, and his charm was no less formidable. His reputation as a lover was such that half

the ladies in London seemed to be intent upon beginning a
liaison with him, but for Lady Alabeth Manvers there
would be no difficulty at all in finding her way into his
arms—she would only have to beckon and he would be
there. But was that what she wanted? Did she even
consider this possibility now because she found him attractive for himself, or did she really consider it, as Piers
Castleton had said, because she saw in him the image of
her dead love? Whatever it was, Piers had been right about
one thing: she was at risk.

The landau was coming nearer to Carlton House now
and there were interested onlookers lining the way, staring
in open admiration at the elegantly clothed ladies and
gentlemen en route to the capital's grand night. Jillian was
positively fidgeting with excitement when at last the
Prince's residence came into sight behind its Ionic colonnade. Outwardly Carlton House was unremarkable, but it
was set in beautiful, extensive gardens which stretched the
length of Pall Mall as far as the wall of Marlborough
House. They were natural and informal grounds, as
fashion now dictated, and they were noted for some
particularly magnificent elms, some charming bowers and
grottoes, a waterfall, a temple with an Italian marble floor,
and an observatory. Now, in the fading evening light, they
were ablaze with little colored lanterns, and it was like
looking into fairyland itself.

It seemed that the landau would never turn into the
courtyard, where a band was playing, but eventually it was
maneuvering between the columns and drawing to a long-
awaited standstill by the dignified Corinthian portico. Servants, wearing the Prince's livery of dark blue trimmed
with gold lace, were waiting to assist the guests to alight,
and Alabeth and Jillian stepped down onto a sprinkling of
scented moss and rose petals, to be escorted up to the open
doors by two liveried Negroes carrying flaming torches.

There were lanterns everywhere, shining down from the

portico and twinkling beneath the colonnade, and the music from the band was vying a little with that of the orchestra playing in the ballroom. Members of the Prince's household received them in the magnificent hall where more Ionic columns, this time of brown Siena marble, lined the way to an octagon from which rose a graceful double staircase to the state apartments above. The walls were hung with an impressive number of the Prince's prized Dutch paintings, and high above was a chandelier of such opulence that Jillian gazed at it in wonder.

The whole house was beautifully and expensively furnished, the pieces mostly chosen by the Prince himself. The French influence, thought by many to have been most undesirable while the war endured, was in evidence everywhere: in the pictures, girandoles, clocks, looking glasses, the bronzes, the Sevres china, the Gobelin tapestries, and the many other *objets d'art* which combined to make up this fabulous place. All in all, it was a little too ornate for Alabeth—she much preferred the Tudor style of Charterleigh—but Jillian thought it quite exquisite and told the Prince as much when she was presented to him a moment later. She could not have said anything more calculated to make him pleased, and he had beamed at her, pronouncing her a most delightful creature, most delightful.

Like Almack's, His Royal Highness had not come up to scratch as far as Jillian was concerned, for although he was handsome and charming, he was also exceedingly fat and not at all her notion of how the first Prince of Europe should look. Behind her fan, she informed Alabeth that he was most unwise to wear such tight-fitting pantaloons, and that to have a coat which fitted him like a glove was surely the very last thing a gentleman of his proportions should be doing. Alabeth was thankful when they were well and truly out of royal earshot, for Jillian's stage whisper would have done justice to Drury Lane.

The ballroom was immense and illuminated by myriads

of candles. There was a great deal of noise, both from the orchestra and from the hundreds of guests, and Alabeth soon perceived a number of French voices, proof positive that half Paris was in London and half London in Paris. A sea of ostrich plumes waved beneath the chandeliers, jewels flashed, orders gleamed on black velvet, and the French guests of honor were arrayed on scarlet and gold sofas, looking as grand as the Bourbons they had striven to overthrow so bloodily.

As Alabeth and Jillian neared the sofas, they saw quite suddenly that one of the English gentlemen speaking with the French Ambassador was Piers Castleton. Like most of the gentlemen present, he wore black velvet, and he looked relaxed and graceful, conversing easily in French. At that moment, as if he sensed their presence, he turned, but his glance was only vaguely interested as he gave them an unsmiling bow.

Jillian uneasily returned the bow with a curtsy, Alabeth matched his coolness by merely inclining her head and then walking on. There, it was done, the dreaded moment was over and she had conducted herself with style, but her pulse was racing and all she could think of was the way he had pulled her close and kissed her. She held her head high, pushing the memory from her mind. She wouldn't let it bother her, she *wouldn't!*

He passed from their sight as they mingled with the throng of people, searching for Octavia and the party they were to join. Charles Allister was also of the party, and his delight at being greeted so pleasantly by Jillian was quite touching. Encouraged, he remained close by her side from that moment on, making his displeasure quite plain to every gentleman who made so bold as to ask her to dance, but it wasn't until the subject of the Count came up in conversation that his smile most definitely faded.

"The fellow may play the pianoforte perfectly, but he plays cards *im*perfectly," he declared, glancing almost defiantly at Jillian, who had been once again praising the Count's many virtues.

Octavia was appalled. "Oh, surely you are mistaken!"

"I'm convinced he was palming cards, but I could not catch him at it. If I do, I'll—"

Octavia tapped his arm reprovingly with her fan. "By your own admission you didn't catch him doing anything, so until you do, you had better keep a still tongue in your head, sir, for it isn't done to call another gentleman a sharp unless you have proof. Come now, Charles, it isn't like you to be so hotheaded."

"I don't care for the fellow."

"That much is obvious," Octavia replied, glancing at Jillian. "And I believe we know why."

Jillian flushed a little and fidgeted with her fan. Charles continued to look stormy, quite unable to be placid where the Count, whom he obviously regarded as a rival, was concerned.

Alabeth smiled at him. "I do believe I hear a cotillion being announced, Charles, and I am sure Jillian would be delighted to dance with you."

He smiled then. "Am I being a bear?"

"You are."

"Forgive me, I shall endeavor to improve. Lady Jillian, will you honor me with this dance?"

She accepted his hand and they went to join the other dancers on the floor. Octavia sat back thoughtfully. "I detect a definite improvement in her of late, Alabeth. Has she come around at last?"

"Oh, yes."

"And is she viewing Charles with favor?"

"That I don't know."

"Hmm. Well, we must hope. Now, then, I've been meaning to ask you about the arrangements for her ball. I've been thinking that it would be good to . . ." Octavia launched into her extravagant notions for Jillian's great day, and Alabeth listened, hardly having to add a single word, because it was obvious that Octavia had it all settled in her mind and the ball was as good as arranged.

The dance ended and Jillian and Charles returned to the sofa, which Octavia had deliberately chosen as it was a considerable vantage point from which to survey the whole room. Octavia's fan was raised now to conceal her lips and she leaned conspiratorily toward Alabeth. "Have you seen our fashionable impure?"

"Who?"

"Why, Lady Adelina Carver, of course, over there, slightly to the side of the orchestra. In virginal white from head to toe." This last was said with considerable acidity.

Adelina's full-bosomed figure was quite easy to pick out, for she was very tall and wore immense plumes, which made her even taller. There was too much rouge on her lips, her gown revealed too much bosom, and it was so flimsy that when she moved it was quite possible to see her long legs.

Octavia sniffed. "She's given Seaham his marching orders once and for all and he's totally devastated, foolish fellow. How he couldn't see that he was but one of many, I'll never know, but then men ever were fools in that direction, weren't they? She arrived very early on and attached herself to Harry Ponsonby—he's over the other side of the room, the one in Guards uniform by that column, d'you see him?"

Alabeth nodded, glancing at the slender young officer with his soft brown eyes and winning smile.

"Well," went on Octavia with relish, "they stayed together for a little while, she clinging to him like a vine, but then they had a tiff and he walked off, nose in the air, and he's refused to glance at her ever since. She's done everything to catch his attention, but he's not having any of it, and now she looks fit to burst into tears at any moment—and serve her right."

"How very sympathetic you are."

"She's had a veritable string of lovers and has been disgracefully indiscreet with all of them, Seaham included. It would be bad enough had she been a married woman, but she is not and so her sins are all the greater."

"Oh, Octavia—"

"Alabeth, I am set upon this. There are rules which should be observed, and Adelina Carver observes none of them. There is no discretion whatsoever and I find that quite unacceptable. This business with Ponsonby may possibly be a little different, for I do believe the chit actually loves him, but she will receive scant sympathy from society because of her atrocious conduct in the past."

"I feel rather sorry for her," Alabeth said, "for it is quite obvious that she is very unhappy." She looked across the room at the sad eyes of the woman who had more than earned her reputation.

"*Sorry* for her? How could you, Alabeth!" Octavia looked a little taken aback and a little cross, and she was visibly relieved when at that moment dinner was announced. She turned to Jillian and Charles. "I wonder what Prinny's chefs have concocted for our jaded palates? Come along, *mes enfants,* let us go and see." Ushering them before her, she bustled away, obviously not well pleased with Alabeth for even remotely defending Adelina Carver.

Alabeth remained where she was for a moment, thinking how unlike Octavia it was to be so cold and hard. It could only be that Seaham's infidelities over the years had hurt her far more than she had ever admitted. At last Alabeth joined the crowds moving in the direction of the great conservatory, where the dinner was to be served, and all around her she could hear as many French voices as English. She wondered wryly what her father would have made of this gathering of Bonapartists in the London palace of the Prince of Wales.

15

The immense Gothic convervatory was perhaps Carlton House's crowning glory. Designed like a cathedral, it had a nave and two aisles, and in daytime was very airy and light because of its glazed tracery ceiling, but now it was lighted artificially and the shadows beyond the light were curving and elegant. Lanterns had been placed on the outside to illuminate the stained-glass windows with their heraldic arms of the sovereigns of England, the Princes of Wales, and the Electoral Princes of the House of Brunswick. Inside, innumerable colored lights had been placed in niches and there were hexagonal lanterns suspended from the points of the arches.

A table two hundred feet long and covered with snowy-white cloths had been laid out; it was so long that it extended the length of the conservatory and into the house itself. In front of the raised seats where the Prince and his guests of honor would sit there was a silver fountain surrounded by perfume-burning vases, and from it flowed a stream of water which passed along a little canal raised about six inches above the cloths. The banks of this stream were decorated with green moss and flowers and there were silver and gold fish darting in the water. The murmur of the water was soothing, a welcome relief after the noise of the ballroom.

The Prince led the way, obviously gratified at the admiration the dining arrangements were receiving from all sides, and when everyone was seated, it was toward the dais that every eye was inexorably drawn by the succession of blazing candelabra. There the Prince sat in splendor, his large figure standing out against a background of crimson velvet on which was embroidered a golden crown and the initials GR.

Alabeth found the place marked with her name on a little card, and a footman drew the chair out for her. As she sat down, she saw Octavia making mental notes concerning the decorations. Their eyes met for a moment and Octavia gave her a rueful smile, unable to remain in a miff with her for very long.

Glancing around, Alabeth saw Piers entering the conservatory, and on his arm was Adelina Carver, smiling very brightly indeed as she kept her eyes averted from Harry Ponsonby, who was accompanied by a daring French lady whose gown was even more revealing and shameless than Adelina's. Piers leaned toward her, whispering something in her ear, and Adelina's tinkling laughter rang out audibly. Harry scowled as they passed him, Adelina not even seeming to notice his presence.

Piers was very attentive indeed, drawing out Adelina's chair for her himself and then deliberately replacing the card placed next to her with his own. Only once in those moments did Adelina glance at Harry, whose back was firmly turned toward her, and for a second Alabeth thought she saw the former unhappiness on her face, but then it had gone as Piers murmured something to her, smiling as he raised her gloved hand to his lips. She smiled too, her eyes very warm, and after that Alabeth did not see her look once in Harry's direction. Alabeth lowered her eyes to the little fish in the canal. Maybe Octavia had been right to condemn Adelina after all, for she appeared to have moved on to her next lover with quite bewildering swiftness and ease.

Course followed course as the feast began, a procession of tureens, silver domes, plates, and dishes, and all the while the iced champagne flowed as freely as the water from the fountain. By the time the fruit was served at the

end, Alabeth was simply not able to do justice to the
peaches, grapes, and pineapples served so exquisitely on a
bed of leaves. She had been determined to put Piers Castleton from her mind, noting with relief that not once during
the feast did he glance at Jillian or Jillian at him. Indeed
Jillian seemed quite engrossed in whatever it was that
Charles Allister was talking about—amateur theatricals
no doubt, if his animated expression was anything to go
by. Well, thought Alabeth, at least one good thing has
come out of the disagreeable visit to Piers Castleton, for he
had obviously decided to abide by her wishes. She looked
at him again, remembering the semblance of righteous
anger with which he had denied her accusations; and yet all
the time he knew he had exchanged intimate letters with
Jillian, he had met her secretly, and he had been conducting an affair which had more than justified Alabeth's
request that he refrain from any further contact. How
odious he was, and yet as she looked at him now, she still
could not help thinking how handsome and charming he
was. He was looking at Adelina, his lips teasing with that
particular half-smile of his, and his gray eyes were cares-
sing her warmly. How accomplished a lover he was, with
what ease and skill did he set about seducing Adelina.
Alabeth turned her head away, her glance falling on the
silver dish of fruit nestling among the fresh green leaves.
Incongruously she remembered a mellow September
evening at Charterleigh, when she had strolled in the
orchard with Piers and he had picked an apple for her.
Never had an apple tasted so good.

Shortly afterward, the Prince and his guests adjourned
once more to the ballroom, where in a little while the
Count was to play for them all. Alabeth smiled as the
gentleman next to her drew out her chair for her, but as she
turned, she found herself looking straight into Piers' eyes
as he performed a similar task for Adelina. They looked at
each other for a long moment before she coolly walked

away from her place, accepting the arm of General Sir John Fitzwilliam, who had been seated close to her throughout the meal.

She sat on the sofa in the ballroom, watching everyone return from the conservatory. The Prince and his guests were already in their places, all looking very full and very contented after the feast. Alabeth was just beginning to wonder where Octavia, Jillian, and Charles were when her attention was jerked away from the far door by someone addressing her.

"Good evening, Alabeth."

She looked up into Piers' mocking eyes and her face was immediately cold. "Sir."

"I note that your manners have not improved."

"If that is your opinion, I wonder that you bother to approach me."

"Perhaps I am an eternal optimist."

Deliberately she averted her head, intending to force him to go away by ignoring him, but he had no intention of letting her do that.

"Will you honor me with this dance, Alabeth?" he inquired smoothly, a hint of mockery in his tone.

"I would as soon dance with a toad."

"Alas, there are no toads present, so I ask you again. Will you dance with me?"

She gritted her teeth furiously. "Please go away!"

"No, Alabeth, for I intend to have my revenge upon you. Now, then, if you continue to be disagreeable, you will draw even more attention from His Royal Highness than you are at present, and that would not do at all, would it?" He spoke, oh, so reasonably, smiling all the while.

Her glance fled to the Prince, who was indeed watching them, his quizzing glass swinging idly in his plump fingers.

"You see?" went on Piers. "So I rather think you had better accept my invitation, don't you?"

"I despise you," she whispered, knowing that she really had no choice, for she could hardly risk offending the Prince by her conduct.

"I don't really care what you think of me," he murmured, still smiling. "I only care that you shall not get away with paying me visits such as the one on the day after Octavia Seaham's ball. Now, then, shall we dance?"

His expression was satirical as he led her onto the floor, but her face was wooden; she could neither smile nor scowl, she was too angry. By forcing her into dancing with him, he was indeed extracting an exquisite revenge, for he knew he was making her behave in a way which went very much against the grain.

At last the final notes died away and she made to leave him immediately but he held her hand, drawing it firmly through his arm. "No, Alabeth, you will walk politely from the floor with me, on that I am determined."

"Please let me go, sir, you have had your sport."

"I have had a little revenge for the disgraceful way you have seen fit to treat me."

Her cheeks were flames now. "Your conduct is singularly lacking in any gentlemanly qualities, sirrah," she breathed, being careful all the while to look as composed as possible.

"Is it indeed?" he inquired mildly. "And here am I congratulating myself upon being a perfect angel for you, doing my best to comply with your strange request that I stop pursuing your sister. Why, I haven't even spoken to her, for fear you would accuse me of ravishing her. Really, I think it is impossible for me to please you, Alabeth, for whatever I do, you still find fault. You have sadly changed, for I recall that once you were the sweetest, most beautiful, and most delightful of creatures—"

"Don't you dare to speak to me anymore, sir, for I find everything about you most offensive—and obscenely dishonest!"

His smile faded at that, and his hand tightened over her fingers as she tried to extricate herself from his grasp. "And what do you mean by that last remark?" he asked coldly.

"I think you know well enough!" She glanced around a little self-consciously, praying that their low, urgent exchange was not being remarked unduly.

"I know no such thing—pray tell me."

"Very well. At our last meeting you scornfully denied having any improper intentions toward my sister, you spoke very righteously about your innocence, but I know full well that you were lying, sirrah. You were indeed pursuing her and had been doing so since meeting her at Chatsworth last year. Oh, you are a skillful lover, Piers Castleton, knowing full well that she was innocent and inexperienced and totally unused to the ways of gentlemen such as yourself."

"You are wrong," he said icily. "As wrong about this as you seem to be wrong about everything else."

"Am I? I suppose you will deny meeting her secretly at Wallborough—just as you will deny exchanging indiscreet letters with her, one of which was intercepted. I know the truth about you, sir, which makes your conduct tonight all the more reprehensible and low. Now, will you let me go?"

His face was dark and angry, but he released her. He appeared not to trust himself to speak, and they looked bitterly into each other's eyes before she turned to walk away, her head held high and her cheeks still fiery. She felt at once furious with him and dismayed with herself. Her fury was brought about by his infamous conduct, her dismay by the fact that she had allowed herself to be goaded into mentioning Jillian's letter. She remembered Jillian's anxiety about the letter being mentioned and her overwhelming relief on discovering that it hadn't. Oh, damn him, *damn* him! Alabeth could have wept, for although she could not see why the letter should make any difference, she felt that she had let Jillian down by speaking of it with him.

Octavia was seated on the sofa when she returned to take her place, but there was no sign of Jillian or Charles. Octavia's glance was thoughtful. "And what was all that about?"

"All what?"

"The restrained but heated exchange with Piers Castleton."

"Nothing."

"Indeed? I hate to think what it could have been like had there been something," remarked Octavia drily, her fan wafting to and fro as she watched Piers walk toward Adelina, who was seated at the far side of the room. "Whatever that nothing was, it certainly has aroused him, for he is being positively ferocious with that unfortunate Frenchman who happened to brush against him."

Unwillingly Alabeth turned to look. The Frenchman looked quite taken aback at Piers' unwarranted anger, but was obviously anxious to smooth the whole thing over, for he bowed and apologized most handsomely. Piers moved on, catching Adelina's eye and smiling suddenly, his anger seeming to evaporate. She stood, he drew her hand gently through his arm, and they strolled away into the crowd.

Octavia pursed her lips. "Now there's a strange twosome, don't you think?"

"I have no opinion on the matter."

"No? Oh, well— Still, it *is* strange, for I could have sworn that for once in her wretched life Adelina was truly in love, but Harry Ponsonby was obviously just another conquest. It is also strange because I never would have imagined that she was Piers Castleton's sort—no, not in the slightest. One thing can always be said of him, and that is that he is discreet—Adelina is the very opposite." Octavia's glance was sly then. "Do you still feel sorry for her?"

"I feel sorry for anyone who is taken in by Sir Piers Castleton," remarked Alabeth coolly.

At that moment they were rejoined by Jilllian and Charles, who had been delayed by the Prince as they emerged from the conservatory. Jillian was obviously in seventh heaven, enjoying the gala evening far more than she had ever dreamed possible. Her behavior was impeccable too, for although she had been a great deal in Charles' company, she had not set a foot wrong, having danced with him only once and having conducted herself immaculately throughout. This new Jillian had obviously enslaved Charles forever, for he could not take his eyes from her, and had she asked him for the moon, he no doubt would have attempted to get it for her.

16

Over the next hour or so Alabeth managed to forget the unpleasantness with Piers and set about enjoying herself. She danced with a succession of partners, including the French Ambassador himself, although she doubted if he would have been so gallant had he known of her father's secret mission in Madras.

At last the moment came when the pianoforte recital was announced, and everyone moved toward the rows of seats which the footmen were setting out by the dais. The Prince and his guests occupied the sofas placed directly before the pianoforte, and Octavia scuttled with almost indecent haste to sit herself squarely in the middle of the only remaining sofa in the front row, turning to beckon urgently to Alabeth and Jillian to join her. Alabeth was conscious of a flutter of anticipation as she sat down, carefully arranging her skirts.

Octavia smiled sleekly. "Now we shall see how much of a conquest you have made, Alabeth Manvers, for he cannot fail to see you right here in the front."

Alabeth said nothing, but her pulse was racing a little as she heard the first stir as the Count entered the ballroom and approached the pianoforte, pausing to give a deep bow before the Prince, who nodded graciously. The Count wore russet, an intricate, soft cravat spilling from his throat, and his legs encased in pale pantaloons. His hair looked very golden beneath the brilliance of the chandeliers, and his eyes looked almost sapphire as he glanced momentarily over the audience before taking his place at the pianoforte. As he sat down, adjusting his lace cuffs, his eyes rested on Alabeth's pale face. A strange breathlessness held her as their eyes met—his as blue as Robert's had been, and as warm. Her feelings were mixed and confusing as she watched him prepare to play. The ballroom was quiet; not a soul moved.

Once again his skill was bewitching, a display of fire tempered with elegance and control. Music which everyone had heard before seemed like a new composition, so different and exquisite was his interpretation. There was nothing restrained about the sound which flowed over the rapt audience, for when he played with vigor, the whole room was carried along with him, and when he played softly, a thrill ran through them all. His long, pale fingers moved gently over the keys then, as if he took them all into his confidence, to tell them his secret thoughts, but it was to Alabeth alone that his music whispered. Time and time again his eyes moved toward her as he played, and there was no mistaking the ardency or meaning of those glances.

A stir began to pass vaguely through the audience, and even the Prince leaned forward to look at her. As if he sensed that he had been a little too obvious, the Count launched directly into a fiery scherzo which drew all attention back to the music. Alabeth lowered her eyes, conscious of how hot her cheeks were and of how her pulse raced still.

Beside her, Jillian was totally engrossed in the magnificence of the playing. She sat on the edge of the sofa, straining to watch his hands as they flew over the ivory keys, and she was so lost in admiration that she seemed for the moment to have forgotten where she was. As the music ended with a final flourish, she was on her feet, clapping ecstatically and so carried along by the moment that she hurried forward, stepping onto the dais as the Count rose from the pianoforte. He looked a little startled as Jillian hurried toward him, the jeweled comb in her hair flashing and her beautiful shawl dragging along the floor behind her as it slipped from one arm.

"Oh, Count Zaleski, you were superb! Divine!" she cried. "I have never in my life heard such music!"

"You are too kind, *mademoiselle,*" he began, a little taken aback by her unbridled enthusiasm and by the fact that she had appeared to have forgotten that the Prince of Wales was expected to be the first to congratulate him, that having been previously arranged.

Jillian was unaware as yet of the mistake she was making. "Please say that you will give me some tuition, sir," she begged, "for I have quite set my heart upon it."

The applause had dwindled away to nothing now as everyone looked on in amazement at Jillian's incredible behavior, and the Prince did not seem at all pleased. Alabeth was transfixed with horror, taken totally by surprise and unable to think of anything to say or do to smooth the matter over. Jillian at last seemed to become aware of the stir she had caused, and her face drained of color as she turned to look at the sea of faces gazing dumbfounded at her. Her lips began to quiver a little and her huge eyes filled with tears, for the folly was entirely of her own creation and she was unwittingly guilty of a flagrant breach of protocol, and in front of the Prince of Wales himself!

Charles Allister looked so upset for her that Alabeth feared he was about to make the whole matter worse by rushing up to Jillian and taking her in his arms.

At last Alabeth found her wits, stepping forward to curtsy low before the Prince. "Your Royal Highness, I must beg you to forgive my sister, for I fear she has been quite carried away, first by the magnificence of the evening and now by the excellence of the music."

Her words reminded him of how ecstatic had been Jillian's admiration for Carlton House, and he was a little mollified. "Perhaps her enthusiasm is understandable," he murmured.

Alabeth threw a meaningful glance at her sister, and Jillian belatedly observed the rules, sinking into a quite beautiful curtsy. "Forgive me, Your Royal Highness, for I am guilty of the most awful sin."

He smiled at that. "Awful sin? My sweet Lady Jillian, how could such an angel as you have ever sinned?" He glanced around, smiling still and thus signifying his forgiveness. To Alabeth's intense relief, the dreadful silence was at an end and everyone began to murmur again.

After a few words with the Count, the Prince and his guests adjourned to their sofas again, the Prince asking a footman to bring him some maraschino, and at last Alabeth could turn to the Count herself. "Please accept my apologies, sir."

"There is no need for you to apologize, Lady Alabeth," he replied, bowing very gallantly.

Jillian spoke up swiftly. "Maybe not, sir, but there is every need for me to do so. My conduct was dreadful and I do not deserve the kindness of either His Royal Highness or yourself. I am very ashamed of myself and can offer only the excuse that I was totally enthralled by your music."

He smiled. "Ah, Lady Jilllian, how very flattering you are."

"I do not flatter you, sir, for that would imply that I give more praise than your genius deserves. I have never before heard such music, it was as if a whole orchestra were playing."

He nodded, looking at her with some interest. "It pleases me immensely that you should describe it so, for it is my belief that the pianoforte is the only complete instrument—through its notes the whole range of expression is possible."

"Oh, yes, yes!" she agreed. "I have always felt that that

is so, but I have never been able to produce music of such quality as I have heard tonight."

"You are, I see, a serious musician, Lady Jillian."

"I like to think that I am, sir."

"Then I would indeed be delighted to give you the tuition you requested."

She could hardly believe her ears. "You would?"

"But of course."

"I do not know how to thank you."

"You may thank me by proving to be a pupil who pays attention at all times and who, above all else, learns greatly from what I have to say."

"I will, I promise that I will."

"I will call upon you—" He broke off, for at that moment Charles Allister appeared at Jillian's elbow, deliberately drawing her hand through his arm and beginning to remove her from the Count's presence, murmuring something about having someone he very much wished to introduce her to. As he walked away, he cast back a look of pure loathing at the Count, and received by way of reply a glance of immeasurable chill from the Pole's blue eyes.

Alone with the Count, Alabeth felt quite shocked by the silent exchange between the two men. She cleared her throat a little uncomfortably. "I, er, see that you and Sir Charles are acquainted, sir."

"We are, but he has insulted me, and that I do not forgive," he replied softly and in a way which made her shiver a little. He seemed to recover a little from his anger then, for he smiled at her. "Forgive me, Lady Alabeth, for that was churlish of me. May I make amends by asking you to dance again?"

"It would be in order, sir, but I fear that I have danced enough tonight."

"Then walk awhile with me in the gardens."

"Oh, I don't know—"

"Please . . . or are you afraid of me, perhaps?"

"Afraid? No."

"Then walk with me," he said softly, offering her his arm.

The gardens were bathed in moonlight and the trees and walks twinkled with little lanterns. Covered walks had been constructed for the evening, decorated with flowers and mirrors and intersected by other walks where a number of guests strolled, but the Count preferred the open lawn. Her train dragged across the cool grass where peacocks strutted and where not a single daisy dared to show its pale face amid the flawless green. The silent statues watched and the sounds of the city all around were distant, as were the faint strains of a minuet from the ballroom.

The air was sweet with the perfume of flowering shrubs and herbs, from the orange blossom and roses to the freshness of lavender and rosemary. The Count led her toward a little summer house entwined with honeysuckle, and she sat down inside, gazing over the expanse of the beautiful gardens before her.

He touched the apricot colored honeysuckle with a fingertip. "There was such a plant as this on my estate near Warsaw."

"You must miss your country very much."

"I do, but one day I will return."

"Do you have family there still?"

"My family was all killed, Lady Alabeth, they were among ten thousand slain by the Russians at Praga, Warsaw."

She stared at him in horror. "Oh, how dreadful—"

"My estate and my family, all taken by the enemies of my country." There was little of the civilized Frenchman about him now; he was a Polish patriot, filled with all the emotion of his people.

"I'm so sorry," she whispered.

"Bonaparte and the French will free my country again, Lady Alabeth, of that I am certain."

"Is that why you went to Paris?"

"Yes. Did you know that there is a prophecy in Poland which says that when all things are falling apart and wickedness is rife in the world, then a second Frankish Charles will rise as Emperor to purge and heal and bring back peace to the world?"

"And you believe the First Consul to be this Charlemagne?" she asked, remembering her father's words at Charterleigh.

"Yes, I do."

"But would it be right for one man to have such power?"

He smiled. "Oh, how very English you sound, my lady."

"Forgive me."

"I would forgive you anything," he said softly, "anything at all."

The atmosphere changed subtly and she rose slowly to her feet. "Perhaps we should go inside again."

"Why?"

"Because we have been here some time."

"Five minutes?" His glance was teasing. "Hardly a long time."

"It is not gentlemanly to put obstacles before a lady, sir."

"I do not wish to be a gentleman, Lady Alabeth, I wish to be your lover."

Her breath caught at such directness. "You should not say such a thing—"

"Would you prefer me to be dishonest?"

"I would prefer you to be less forward."

"I do not pretend to know the intricacies of your English ways, but I do know that I find you the most beautiful and desirable of women and that I am determined to conquer you.''

"I will not be *conquered* by anyone, sir,'' she replied, but her heart began to pound as he touched her cheek with the finger which a moment before had caressed the honeysuckle.

"My first name is Adam,'' he said softly. "There should be no formality between us.''

"You go too fast! By far too fast!''

"No, I think not. Your heart is the prize,'' he murmured, "and whether I lay seige to it or take it by storm, in the end it will be mine.''

She knew that he was going to kiss her and she did not know whether she wished it or not. She was trapped by a web of memories, memories which even now made her think fleetingly of Robert, who had had the same golden hair and the same warm blue eyes— But then Piers' scornful voice was echoing in her head. "It was very much a flesh-and-blood Polish aristocrat with your seduction on his mind . . . Be under no illusion about Zaleski, for it could be your undoing . . . You are at risk, Alabeth, because you have made yourself vulnerable to Robert's memory. . . .''

She drew back sharply. "I wish to return to the house now.''

He saw that he would progress no further for the time being, and he smiled charmingly. "Very well.''

To her relief, he offered her his arm and they walked back across the lawns toward the nearest of the covered walks, but as they entered, they both halted, for they distinctly heard the sound of a woman weeping. Then, in one of the mirrors, Alabeth saw the reflection of Adelina Carver, crying as if her heart were breaking as she clung to Piers. He held her close, his fingers coiling lovingly in her hair.

Alabeth hurried on, the Count hesitating only a moment

before following her. Once back in the ballroom, he was spirited away from her immediately by numerous admirers, and she made her way back to Octavia's sofa, hoping that she looked a good deal more composed than she felt.

Octavia's fan wafted slowly to and fro. "Well?"

"Well, what?"

"Don't be infuriating, you know perfectly well what. You've made *the* conquest, we're all furiously jealous, and all you can say is 'Well, what?' I trust he made very improper suggestions to you in the gardens."

"You are incapable of reforming, aren't you?"

"Did he?"

"Yes."

"Good."

"Good?"

"My dear, he's delectable, good enough to eat, and he's offering himself on a silver plate. Don't tell me you aren't even going to nibble."

"You would, I suppose."

"Naturally. Since I did my duty and provided Seaham with two sons, I've been nibbling away here and there to my heart's content. You should be doing the same, for it would do you good."

"You may be right."

"I *am* right. Take him for your lover, Alabeth Manvers, and don't be slow about it, for there are a hundred others waiting eagerly to step into your shoes."

Alabeth said nothing.

"By the way, your Aunt Silchester has sent a message through one of her tabby friends."

"Oh."

"Well you might 'oh,' for she is not pleased with you."

"What have I done?"

"It's what you haven't done that's more to the point. You haven't called upon her, and as she considers herself to be the matriarch of the family, she ain't too delighted."

"I suppose I should have called before now," admitted Alabeth.

"You should, indeed, especially as her scouts inform her of all the other calls you *have* managed to make. It was most foolishly remiss of you, for now you've given the old biddy something to really gripe about."

Alabeth sighed.

Octavia smiled. "Still, an hour or so with your Aunt Silchester can be endured, especially as there's Ascot week to look forward to, to say nothing of my boating party. Cheer up, Alabeth, just think of languishing in the Count's arms and you'll come through anything."

Alabeth laughed then. "Oh, Octavia!"

17

Jillian looked very pretty indeed as she set out to dine at Lady Dexter's, and Alabeth could have sworn that she was pleased at the notion of being seated next to Charles Allister again. It hardly seemed possible that such a change could have come about, but it had, and Alabeth even began to hope that her father's dearest wish was coming true and that there would indeed be a match between his younger daughter and the son of his greatest friend. The Jillian who had greeted Alabeth that first awful evening had not reappeared at all, and it certainly seemed that for some reason the fact that Alabeth had confronted Piers Castleton had brought about a complete transformation. Alabeth still knew a few twinges of guilt for having blurted out about the letters to Piers, but she knew that it could not be undone now and, besides, it really did not matter anymore, for Piers obviously hardly crossed Jillian's mind now.

The Wallborough landau bore Jillian away from the house and Alabeth prepared to call upon Aunt Silchester, a duty which she viewed with extreme dislike, for she and her aunt had never got on, even before the elopement with Robert, and since then relations had been very strained indeed, the old lady never missing an opportunity to upbraid her scandalous niece.

Lady Silchester resided in Baswick Street, which was but a short distance from Berkeley Square, and as the early evening was clear and fine, Alabeth decided to walk, accompanied by a footman for protection, as it would be dusk on her return. She wore a cherry velvet spencer over a pale-pink muslin gown, and on her head a straw bonnet with a posy of flowers pinned to the underbrim. A long ringlet tumbled down over her shoulder and her fringed parasol threw a cool shadow over her as she walked along the pavement toward Gunter's, where a small collection of elegant carriages had already gathered. There was light-hearted laughter and the murmur of idle conversation as the excellent ices and other confections were sampled, and Alabeth exchanged greetings with several people before continuing on her way.

Her mood was light, for she had had a very lazy day after rising very late indeed, and she had spent some hours on the seat beneath the mulberry tree in the garden, enjoying the peace and pondering the events of recent weeks. She felt satisfied that she had dealt correctly with the problem of Piers Castleton, having made her opinion of him quite clear and having at the same time carried out her duties as chaperone to the best of her ability. As far as the Count was concerned, well, she could not help feeling rather flattered at receiving such ardent attention from the man who was adored by nearly every woman in London. How could any woman not be pleased at being pursued by such a man? She was not fool enough to think his intentions were honorable, nor was she really under any illusion about herself, for she knew in her heart that a great deal of his attraction as far as she was concerned was because he reminded her so very much of Robert. Had she been another Adelina, or even an Octavia, then perhaps she would have given in to his advances, but she was not like them and had no intention whatsoever of capitulating. He might be thinking in terms of conquering her, but she was most certainly only thinking in terms of a mild flirtation. At least, that was the firm intention, but when one was alone with him in the moonlight, it was far more difficult to stick to one's intentions.

Her footman escorted her to the door and remained outside as she was admitted. The door closed behind her, shutting out the summer evening so that the stillness of the house seemed to fold over her. Some of her aunt's lapdogs pattered over the tiled floor to greet her, snuffling around her hem and wagging their tails in the hope that she would scoop them up, but there was no time to do any such thing, for she was shown immediately up to her aunt's rather intimidating bedchamber.

Not a single window was open, Aunt Silchester being of the firm belief that fresh air was bad for one's constitution, bringing as it did a variety of ill humors to beset one's stamina. The room was hung with drab damask and the drapes around the heavy, old-fashioned bed were a similar dull color. The evening sunlight was muted by the heavy lace at the windows and the overall impression was rather stifling. Aunt Silchester reposed on a mound of pillows, her wispy white hair almost entirely hidden beneath an enormous day bonnet. A pair of owlish spectacles rested on the end of her pointed nose and there was a look of extreme superiority on her face. Being the Earl of Wallborough's sister, there was a great deal of Carstairs about her, but her expression and manner were pure Silchester, into which vain and pompous family she had married, and she now considered herself to be much more grand than she actually was. However, in the Earl's absence she was undoubtedly the most senior member of the family and, as such, was to be treated with all due respect, her many failings being ignored as if they did not exist.

Her lips twisted a little sourly as Alabeth was shown in. "You've taken your time, missy."

"Forgive me, Aunt Silchester," replied Alabeth, placing a dutiful kiss on the older woman's wrinkled cheek.

"Hm. Well, you're looking healthy enough, although I cannot say I approve of your having discarded mourning after only two years, even for a fellow like Manvers. Three years is the accepted time in the Silchester family."

Alabeth sat down. "I trust you are feeling a little better now."

"If I am, it's no thanks to those cursed quacks. They've dosed me up with physic, bled me, purged me, advised the waters at Bath, concocted all manner of foul medicaments, and I'm increasingly convinced that had they left me alone I would have recovered in good time to do my duty by your sister. I certainly do not know that I am in agreement with Wallborough that you are equipped for the task, Alabeth."

"I am doing my best," replied Alabeth sweetly, doing her best indeed to remain calm before such insults.

"Hm. I think Jillian is looking particularly pretty. She'll make a good catch, and no mistake."

"Yes."

"And I am told that Charles Allister is very smitten."

"He is."

"Hm. Well, in the absence of a suitable scion of the house of Silchester, no doubt an Allister will have to do."

She spoke as if the Silchesters were princes of the blood, thought Alabeth, still smiling sweetly. "Charles is a considerable match, Aunt Silchester, and Jillian could do a lot worse than snap him up."

"Well, no one could do worse than you did, missy, and that's a fact."

"No doubt."

"I still cannot understand how you could take a wastrel like Manvers as your husband, Alabeth, charming as he may have been. In my day one didn't *marry* handsome rogues; one married dull fellows like the Duke of Treguard and then took the likes of Manvers as lovers. That was a far more acceptable way of going about it, but you had to turn your back on a match with a Duke and run away with the fellow whose reputation left a great deal to be desired. I nearly washed my hands of you, for the notoriety you attached to the family name was quite odious."

Alabeth said nothing to all this, for she had heard it countless times before and had learned that the best way of dealing with it was not to rise to the bait.

Aunt Silchester sniffed. "Hm. Well, you must understand that I cannot but be alarmed that you have charge of your sister's first Season, for you cannot run your own life to any satisfaction and therefore cannot be expected to run hers either. It is most unfortunate that your sister must embark upon her career in society with the undoubted millstone of your past around her neck."

"I hardly think that it is that bad, Aunt."

"Hm. Well, I think it is, for your conduct recently has hardly inspired confidence."

"My conduct?"

"You are supposed to be setting Jillian an example, but what sort of example is it when you think nothing of walking alone at night with a Russian music-master."

"He's not Russian, he's Polish," replied Alabeth with great forbearance. "And he certainly isn't a music-master, he's a very great musician. Besides, we walked in the gardens at Carlton House and there were a number of other ladies and gentlemen doing the same."

"It was still a far from shining example to set your sister."

Alabeth lapsed into silence, for no matter how much she might protest, she knew that on this occasion her aunt was right; there had been moments in the Prince of Wales' summerhouse which had been far from innocent and which would indeed have been considered reprehensible for a chaperone! Not that Aunt Silchester knew that, she was simply condemning everything from habit as she always did.

"Alabeth, I thoroughly disapprove of such goings-on, and I trust that I shall not hear anything else to cause me concern."

"No, Aunt Silchester." Alabeth gazed out through a

crack in the curtains. The sun was beginning to set now, the sky was turning crimson and gold, and the shadows were lengthening.

"If I do hear anything," her aunt went on relentlessly, "I shall not hesitate to write to your father informing him of the situation."

Alabeth's glance was stony, but she held her tongue, for there was little point in allowing herself to be drawn by this disagreeable old woman who had little else to do with her time but meddle and cause trouble.

Aunt Silchester made herself a little more comfortable in the bed. "Now, then, I am feeling a little sleepy, having not long taken my elixir. The next time you manage to find the time to call upon me, missy, see that you do so at a time when I have not just taken my medication and when there will be more opportunity for polite conversation. You may kiss me." She presented her cheek.

Alabeth rose and obeyed, and a moment later was thankfully escaping from the room where the atmosphere was as suffocating as the so-called polite conversation.

But as she descended the staircase toward the breathlessly still hall, someone rapped at the door with a cane and the footman hurried to open it. She froze as Piers Castleton was admitted. He removed his hat and gloves and handed them to the footman. "I believe that Lady Silchester wished to see me about the sale of an estate in Northumberland—" He broke off, seeing the slight movement on the stairs, and his eyes became noticeably cooler as he saw her. "Good evening, Lady Alabeth."

"Sir." She could not have clipped the word more had she tried.

He waved the footman away. "Do not inform Lady Silchester that I am here just yet."

"No, Sir Piers." The footman cast a nervous glance at Alabeth and then hurried discreetly away, not wishing to become involved in any dispute.

Piers folded his arms, looking coldly at her. "I am glad to have encountered you here, madam, for it saves me the undoubted trouble of calling upon you."

"We have nothing to say to each other," she replied, continuing down the stairs and trying to walk past him to the front door, but he caught her arm and jerked her furiously around to face him.

"We have a great deal to say to each other, madam, whether you like it or not."

"Unhand me!"

He glanced beyond her at a door which stood slightly ajar, and he thrust her toward it, pushing her into the room beyond and then closing the door as he turned to face her. It was the morning room, well away from the sun now, and it smelled of spirit, the windows having been cleaned not long before. Like the rest of the house, it was gloomy and still, almost airless, in fact, and with the door closed as it now was, she felt cut off from the rest of the world.

He stood there, looking at her, his sage-green coat almost gray in the poor light. His eyes were bright with anger. "I told you that I would not grant you any more chances, Alabeth, and I meant what I said. Your conduct at Carlton House was most certainly the last straw, for your wild accusations did not go unheard, a fact which I cannot tolerate. I have always behaved with great patience and with all honor toward you, madam, but for more than two years now I have endured your inexplicable venom. The time has come for those home truths to be brought out into the open, where I now begin to think they should have been all along."

"I must ask you to release me from this room immediately," she said, a little shaken by the controlled force of his anger.

"I will release you when I am good and ready."

"You have no right to detain me against my will."

"I have every right when you continually call my honor into question."

"You have no honor."

"Have a care, madam," he breathed, his eyes flashing, "have a care."

"I despise you," she whispered, backing away a little, "for you are indeed without honor. You have behaved despicably, both now and in the past, and I do not detract one word I have said to you. You, Sir Piers Castleton, are beneath contempt."

Slowly he came toward her, halting so close that his Hessian brushed against the pink muslin of her gown. "Oh, how you take refuge in your sex, Alabeth, for no man would dare to speak to me as you have just done. Time and time again you insult me, knowing full well that if I retaliate, then I would indeed earn a reputation which is beneath contempt."

"If I were a man, I would still say it!"

"Would you? I think not."

"How can you stand there pretending to be a noble innocent when all the time you have conducted yourself most culpably."

"What am I guilty of?" he inquired softly. "For I swear that I have done nothing and I defy you to prove otherwise."

"You attempted most foully to seduce my sister."

"Did I, indeed? Well, I suggest you ask her if that is the case."

"There is no need to ask her, for I already know. You seem remarkably able to forget those letters, sir."

"Ah, yes, the letters. I have never written to your sister, madam, and I never intend to. However, I am perfectly prepared to believe that *she* wrote to me. My experience of your sister's somewhat romantic, fluff-headed character leads me to believe that she is quite capable of putting pen to paper and composing a letter couched in terms of an

affection which did not exist. I'd lay odds that that letter
was never intended to be sent and that she was mortified
when it was found. Knowing her as I now do, madam, I
believe it to be perfectly in keeping that she would brazen it
out rather than suffer the humiliation of admitting the
letter to be a fabrication."

Alabeth stared at him, for there was a definite ring of
truth about what he said, and it certainly would explain
Jillian's huge anxiety about whether the letter had been
mentioned.

"Well," he inquired, "what have you to say?"

"You have offered an explanation which may possibly
have some foundation."

"I can see from your face that you believe it to have a
great deal of foundation."

"Very well, I admit that what you say sounds very
likely."

"Thank you for that small crumb." He sketched a
mocking bow.

"But it in no way excuses your other conduct."

"Ah, so we are back to that." He put his hands on his
hips, surveying her in the gloom. "You cannot ever set it
aside, can you, Alabeth? You must blame me for all that
befell Robert."

"Because you *are* the blame," she cried defiantly.

"I promise you that I am not."

"I cannot and will not believe you."

"That you will not is true, that you cannot is not.
Robert was vain, foolish, hotheaded, deceitful, and con-
niving; he played you false on many occasions and the duel
in which he died was not caused by the turn of a card but
by his having bedded another man's wife."

"No, that is not true," she whispered.

"Every word of it is true."

"What right have you to condemn Robert when you

yourself have killed in a duel? I'll warrant the paltry reason you suggest for Robert was in fact your own.''

''I do not deny killing the Russian, but I defy you to find my reason paltry. The Russian compromised my sister, and he did so for a wager. I admit this now because my sister is dead and cannot be harmed anymore by the truth. The Russian paid dearly for his crime, Alabeth, and I would not shrink from doing it again. If you find that paltry or in keeping with what lay behind Robert's duel, then I am sorry for you.''

''I did not know—''

''There is a great deal you do not know, madam, and even more you refuse to know. By the time he died, I despised Robert, I despised him for his shallow conceit, his callousness toward you—''

''He wasn't,'' she cried. ''He wasn't!''

''He was, damn you, and you have to face the fact. He kept a mistress—did you know that? No, I can see that you didn't. He had also lost vast sums at the gaming table, and the only reason you were spared from discovering the fact is that the night he died he won back an equally large sum —one more day and you would have lost not only your husband, madam, but the roof over your lovely head too.''

She flinched. ''I will not believe it,'' she whispered. ''I will not believe it, for you remained at his side throughout, and if you despised him, then you would not have done so.''

''I remained at his side because I wished to spare you, Alabeth,'' he said softly. ''And spare you I did, for had any other been his second, then the true reason for the duel would certainly have been revealed to you. I did not want you to be hurt any more than you already had been, and so help me I did what I could to soften the blow. I may have despised the man, Alabeth Manvers, but I certainly did not despise his wife.''

She looked away, her lips trembling.

"Robert was not worth your grief, Alabeth; he did not deserve one single tear and certainly deserved even less of your remorse. He was faithless and could be incredibly unfeeling, and only sheer luck prevented you from learning the truth. Or perhaps it was not luck at all, perhaps it was unkind fate, for had you known the truth a little earlier, then you would have been spared your damned conscience."

"No—"

"But, yes, Alabeth, your marriage was a mistake and you know it."

"That isn't true."

"Yes it is, for you suddenly realized that you were the wife of the wrong man, didn't you?"

It was too much, and with a gasp she raised her hand to strike him, but he was too swift, catching her wrist and then twisting her close.

"Damn you, Alabeth, damn you for making me reach this point! You've blamed me over and over and I will not be blamed anymore, for I was guilty of nothing beyond the fact that I held another man's wife in too high regard— and that wife was not indifferent, was she? There lies the source of your conscience, for although you did not betray your marriage vows by even one kiss, you betrayed them over and over again in your thoughts." He released her suddenly. "Well, it's past now, Alabeth, and I believe I've said all that needs to be said. Go, and take your damned conscience with you. I wish to God I'd never set eyes on you and I pray that our meetings in future will be few and far between."

He inclined his head and then turned to walk from the room. In a blur of tears she saw the footman approach him in the vestibule, explaining that Lady Silchester was sleeping. She heard him reply that he would call another time, and then he was gone.

The tears lay damply on her cheeks as she tried to collect herself, but she trembled and fresh tears stung her eyelids. When she closed her eyes, she was at Charterleigh again, on a warm August afternoon, and Robert was presenting her to Piers Castleton. Piers was taking her hand and drawing it to his lips, and she was realizing in that single, breathless moment that nothing was ever going to be the same again.

She had been dishonest with herself and dishonest with him—and now it was too late.

18

It was some time before she felt composed enough to walk back to Berkeley Square, accompanied by the footman, who must have seen her tear-stained face.

She reached the house at last, having run the gauntlet of the select gathering outside Gunter's without having aroused any curiosity, but as she stepped into the hall, she heard the sound of someone playing the pianoforte in the music room. Jillian must have returned early and she would undoubtedly be able to tell that something was wrong.

She turned to Sanderson. "At what time did Lady Jillian return?"

"Lady Jillian has not returned, my lady; it is Count Zaleski who is playing."

"The Count?" Her heart sank.

"He said that he had called to make arrangements for Lady Jillian's tuition, and when he was informed that both you and Lady Jillian were out, he asked if it would be in order for him to inspect the pianoforte, to see that it was tuned and in good order. He said that it seemed a shame for him to waste his evening entirely on a fruitless call. I, er, I said that I did not think you would object, my lady. I trust that I have not acted unwisely."

"No, of course not, it was a sensible decision. I will go up to speak with him directly, but first I will need my maid."

"Very well, my lady."

She went up to her room, wishing that the Count had chosen some other night to call—or perhaps the truth was that it was no accident that he chose this particular night, for it would not be difficult for him to discover that Jillian would be at Lady Dexter's, thus most probably leaving her sister on her own— Yes, the more she thought about it, the more she thought that this was probably the case. She glanced at her reflection in the cheval glass. Tonight nothing could have been further from her thoughts than the prospect of an entanglement with the handsome Pole.

The door of the music room was ajar, and candles had been lit, as it was dark outside now. The soft, moving light glinted on his fair hair as he played, and she stood in the doorway watching him. She did not think that she had ever seen anyone more beautiful than this aristocratic genius who was at once fire and ice, passion and detachment. He was a contradiction, looking so fine and aesthetic, and yet capable of producing music of such force and vigor that it seemed impossible his slender, pale fingers could have the strength.

In the candleglow the likeness to Robert was even more uncanny, and inevitably her thoughts turned to her marriage. Like Adam Zaleski, Robert Manvers had been a contradiction. Capable of an enchanting charm, he had also been able to cut her to the quick with a hurtful word or a careless action. She had glimpsed the truth about him, but she had drawn a veil over it. Tonight Piers Castleton had wrenched that veil aside.

The final notes of music died away and she entered the room. "Good evening, Count Zaleski."

"Ah, Lady Alabeth. Good evening." He rose, taking her hand and drawing it to his lips. "I trust that you do not mind me coming up here, but it seemed nonsensical to go away without at least inspecting the pianoforte."

"And is it in good order?"

He smiled. "Naturally, it is a Broadwood, and very fine indeed."

"You will be able to use it to teach my sister?"

He nodded, his glance resting thoughtfully on the slight marks still visible from her tears. "Have you been crying—?"

She turned to the sheets of music scattered on the top of the pianoforte. "What was it you were playing?"

"It was a sonata composed by a man named Beethoven. You have heard of him?"

"No, I'm afraid not."

"Soon the whole world will know of him."

"If his music is all as magnificent as that sonata, then I think you are right."

"Why have you been crying?" he asked softly.

"You are mistaken."

"Oh, Alabeth," he reproved, "I know that that is not so."

"I don't wish to discuss it."

She did not know that she was toying with her wedding ring, but his glance moved to her agitated fingers. "You have been weeping for your dead lord?"

"I said that I did not wish to discuss it, sir."

He detected the hint of a tremor in her voice. "Very well, I will not speak of it. Come, Alabeth, let me play some more for you, something soothing perhaps." He held out his hand to her, drawing her closer to the pianoforte.

She could feel the danger in the moment, hear the seduction in his voice, and see it in his eyes, but something made her obey. She stood within the glow of the candles, and as he began to play, his irresistible spell began to coil around her with invisible silken threads. She was transfixed by the simplicity of the clear, melancholy music. Outside, she could see the moon rising, as hauntingly beautiful as the music. The poignancy of the moment, filled as it was with half-thoughts, memories, and broken dreams, was too much—just as he intended it should be. She hid her face in her hands and turned away, unable to stem the fresh tears.

In a moment he was on his feet and had come around the pianoforte to her, taking her gently in his arms and holding her close. "Oh, Alabeth," he murmured, "if only you knew how I wish to kiss away those tears—"

"Please leave me," she began, her voice breaking as she tried to move away, but his arms tightened around her.

"Leave you? How could I leave you when your heart is breaking?" His voice was low and he bent his head to kiss her on the lips, his fingers moving in the softness of her hair. "Oh, Alabeth, I desire you more than any other woman."

From the depths of the house she heard the front door close and Jillians' voice greeting Sanderson, and with a rush of relief she pulled sharply away from the embrace. He could see that the spell was broken, and anger darkened his eyes. His lips pressed together and annoyance touched his movements as he turned quickly to the seat at the pianoforte.

Alabeth watched him, the remnants of the spell drifting away forever. How despicable he was, he had thought nothing of using her unhappiness to further his chances of seducing her. He had deliberately and callously chosen music which would affect her, and he had not cared about anything but his own desire.

He sensed that something was suddenly wrong. "Alabeth—?"

"I think, sir, that in future you should keep your distance."

"Oh, but, Alabeth—"

"And do not address me again with such familiarity, Count Zaleski, for I do not like it and will not permit it."

"I know that you are upset—"

"A fact which you would have done better to observe a little earlier. Your conduct here tonight has been monstrous."

He said nothing in reply, for at that moment Jillian came into the room. "Hello, Alabeth. Good evening, Count Zaleski."

Alabeth smiled, giving no hint of the scene which had passed a second before. "Hello, Jillian. And did you have an agreeable evening?"

"I did, indeed. Charles was most entertaining, he really is an excellent actor, you know; I was quite surprised."

The Count had risen to his feet. "You speak of Sir Charles Allister, Lady Jillian?"

"I do." Jillian's eyes were a little speculative as she looked at him, and Alabeth wondered what she was thinking.

He took out his fob watch. "I think it is time I departed, Lady Alabeth, for I am expected at Brooks's."

Jillian's eyes were wide. "You are a wicked gambler, sir?"

"I enjoy to play cards, yes."

She smiled. "Then I wish you well. I am so sorry I was not at home earlier, sir, but I trust it will not be long before you are able to give me my first lesson."

"I fear that I shall be unable to come to you until after Ascot now, but I will call as soon as possible after that."

"That will be excellent," she replied, smiling. "It really is most kind of you to go to all this trouble."

"Not at all, Lady Jillian."

When he had gone, Alabeth turned to Jillian. "And what have you heard?"

"Heard?"

"Come, now, I know you well enough to know that you've heard something about Charles Allister and the Count."

"Well, to be truthful, I have, and it's most interesting. It appears that after the fete last night—or should I say this morning?—a number of gentlemen, including both Charles and the Count, proceeded to Brooks's. They had been at the table for an hour or so when suddenly Charles accused the Count of having palmed an ace, and it took all Piers Castleton's considerable skill to smooth it over and prevent a duel.''

Alabeth was astounded. "Charles actually accused the Count?''

"Yes, and the Count hotly denied it. They are most definitely enemies now.'' Jillian looked thoughtfully away. "It's strange, but I did not think Charles had it in him.''

"Evidently you were wrong.''

"So it seems. Anyway, the outcome of it now is that the Count accuses Charles of being vindictive, and Charles is set upon ridiculing the Count's musical abilities at every opportunity. It's really very childish.''

"Quarrels about honor frequently are.''

Jillian nodded, still looking thoughtful. "I know I should be more enthusiastic about Charles, but I simply can't. Oh, he can be entertaining, especially when he's talking about his amateur theatricals, but I still find him dull and uninteresting on the whole. I want a man to be exciting and different, I want him to be like your Robert, or Piers Castleton—or even the Count.''

"You would be a lot better off with Charles,'' replied Alabeth with some feeling.

"Possibly.''

Jillian went to the pianoforte, leafing through the sheets of music. Alabeth watched her, wondering if it were true that she had made up that letter to Piers. Jillian smiled suddenly. "It says a great deal for Piers that he was able to prevent the duel between Charles and the Count, doesn't it? I mean, imagine the scandal. I don't think the First Consul would have been well pleased, do you?''

"Hardly. Jillian—?'' Alabeth hesitated to ask.

"Yes?''

"Why did you write that letter to Piers?''

Jillian's smile faded and she put the music sheets down.

"You know that it was all make-believe, don't you?"

Alabeth said nothing.

Jillian sat down very slowly. "It was all so foolish and reprehensible, Alabeth, and was a prime example of what I meant when I said that I always find it difficult to admit to something when I know I'm in the wrong. After I met Piers at Chatsworth, I simply couldn't put him out of my mind. I suppose really that it was because I met him so suddenly after that business with Captain Francis. Anyway, one afternoon I amused myself by imagining I was the woman he loved." Her cheeks reddened. "I was only pretending, I had no intention whatsoever of sending it, but then Father found it. It was the most embarrassing moment of my life and I simply couldn't bring myself to tell the truth, for the truth was so humilating. Father was anxious to put an end to the whole affair, telling me that Piers was not at all suitable, having been involved in that scandalous duel in which the Russian died, and that was why he set his mind on this being my first Season, for with Piers due to go to Europe . . . I behaved very badly and I knew it, but somehow it only made me more disagreeable, especially toward you. I was ashamed of myself and I was totally devastated when you told me you were going to confront Piers. I was brought up very sharp indeed by that. I said then that I'd learned my lesson, and so I have." She smiled ruefully. "Do you think very badly of me, Alabeth?"

Alabeth went to her, bending to put her arms around her. "No, sweeting, of course not."

"I *was* an odious brat, wasn't I?"

"Yes." Alabeth smiled.

Jillian put her tongue out. "You aren't supposed to agree. It's all rather amusing now, when I think of it, for I do not think Piers would *ever* have looked at me, not if he is drawn to the likes of Adelina Carver. It was all the talk at Lady Dexter's tonight."

"What was?"

"Piers and Adelina. It appears that Adelina has told several of her friends that she loves Piers and he loves her."

"Oh?"

"Well, they were together a great deal at Carlton House, weren't they? Everyone remarked upon it, and from what Adelina herself has said, well . . ." Jillian's fingertips passed gently over the smooth surface of the ivory keys. "I envy her, Alabeth."

"Because she has Piers?"

"No, silly, because she has a man *like* Piers. I want to love and be loved by a man like that, Alabeth. I want it more than anything else in the world." Very softly, she began to play.

Alabeth straightened, looking across at her broken reflection mirrored in the window. Piers had told the truth about the letter, he had told the truth about everything. What a fool she'd been. Well, she was paying the price of her foolishness now, for it was too late and he loved another.

19

The boating party which Octavia had arranged to precede Ascot week was a dazzling affair and further proof that as a hostess the Duchess of Seaham could not be equaled.

Stoneleigh Park, the Seaham ancestral home, was only three miles from Windsor and was therefore admirably placed for London, and Ascot. The ruins of an old abbey made a splendid setting for the magnificent new house straddling the low, south-facing hillside, and the park swept down from the grand terrace to the shallow valley where the lake sparkled in the June sun. In the center of the lake was the island where Charles Allister's masque would be performed in the pavilion and where the guests would repose beneath the trees on yellow velvet cushions. There were arbors of flowers and filmy silk draperies which fluttered gently in the light breeze, and music was provided by the orchestra on the golden barge anchored a little way from the island. The strains of Handel's *Water Music* drifted over the water and provided the perfect accompaniment for the occasion.

The elongated flight of steps descending from the house's grand terrace was adorned with tall white poles holding colorful banners. Hundreds of orange trees and other exotic plants had been placed advantageously on the grass, flowers and garlands decorated the wooden jetty, and there were more flowers in the little boats which were beginning to carry the guests to the island. A little earlier, a procession of footmen had conveyed the famed and exorbitantly priced luncheon hampers from Gunter's, and they now waited in the shade of the island's trees. Countless bottles of iced champagne were in readiness, having been chilled overnight with ice from the icehouse in the heart of the wood to the east of the house.

Alabeth and Jillian waited their turn to be taken across the lake, and they occupied their time by strolling along the water's edge. Jillian was in pale green and Alabeth in lavender, the long lace veil of her jockey bonnet fluttering softly down her back. She had come today with the express intention of at least attempting to tell Piers that she was sorry for her past conduct, but as yet there had been no opportunity—and besides, his liaison with Adelina was causing a great deal of speculation.

Everyone at Stoneleigh Park that day appeared to know of the new *amour,* although naturally enough no one mentioned it within the hearing of Octavia or the Duke, or indeed within the hearing of Harry Ponsonby, whose black expression was very telling indeed of his displeasure at the new state of affairs. Adelina herself was not on Octavia's list, which was hardly surprising, but she might as well have been, for the number of times her name was mentioned. Piers alone appeared to be oblivious to all the interest, and had apparently not spoken once of Adelina.

At last it was time for Alabeth and Jillian to take their places in one of the boats. Alabeth could see Piers approaching with a group of gentlemen, and as she sat down on the cushion-strewn seat, she knew that he would be among the other passengers. As he reached the end of the jetty, however, he glanced at his fob watch and announced that he really did not have time to enjoy Octavia's island feast as he had to return to Town. As he spoke, the only remaining seat was right next to Alabeth; he glanced straight into her eyes, and she felt certain that he had no appointment to keep at all, he was simply avoiding any contact with her. She looked away, trying to hide the immeasurable hurt this snub had dealt her, but then perhaps she deserved it, and he had said that all was past now— But the tears pricked her eyes as the boat cast off and the jetty slipped away behind.

A day later she saw him again, only this time he was accompanied by an obviously adoring Adelina. Charles Allister, fresh from a resounding triumph with his famous masque, had invited Alabeth and Jillian to share his box at the opera, where Mrs. Billington, the renowned singer, was to give a concert. Charles looked very splendid in his formal clothes, a sword at his side and a tricorn hat tucked under his arm, and Jillian looked very eye-catching in a crimson taffeta gown, her short curls hidden beneath a trencher cap of the same color and stitched with pearls. She had deliberated over wearing such a daring and vivid color, having had second thoughts from the outset about the suitability of such a shade for a young lady, but somehow it really did suit her, making her look not wicked, but carefree.

Alabeth wore a turquoise tunic over a low-necked white silk gown, and on her head a turban adorned with aigrettes. After the misery of the boating party, she was determined not to sink further into despair, and so tonight she had set out to be cheerful company, and she succeeded admirably for the first half of the concert. It wasn't until the intermission, when the box was thronged with gentlemen eager to pay court to the Earl of Wallborough's beautiful daughters, that she happened to glance past them all at the box opposite, just in time to see Piers and Adelina take their places.

Adelina wore a very *décolleté* white muslin gown, a great deal of her magnificent bosom being displayed to the admiring glances of gentlemen in nearby seats. She wore rouge and jewels sparkled in her hair, and there was a look in her lustrous eyes which proclaimed to one and all that she was well versed in the art of love. She leaned close to

Piers, her smile warm and inviting, and they appeared totally absorbed in each other. Alabeth's buoyancy evaporated, her smile fading unhappily, and it was all she could do to look attentive as a young gentleman rattled on about a particularly knowing tip for the first race at Ascot the following week.

The concert resumed, but Alabeth could no longer enjoy it, her glance going time and time again to the box opposite. She knew it was foolish to let it hurt her so, but she felt as if her heart were breaking and suddenly she could no longer bear it. Leaning across to Charles, she said that she felt a little hot and would walk awhile in the corridor extending behind the boxes. Hastily he rose to his feet to accompany her, but she bade him stay with Jillian, and a moment later she had escaped to the deserted passage with its elegant line of console tables and wall-hung mirrors.

Slowly she walked up and down, listening to the muffled sound of the concert and thinking about the futility of a love which had at first been forbidden and which must now be forgotten. She paused, looking at herself in one of the mirrors. The heartbreak was written very large in her green eyes and in the air of sadness which pervaded her. Oh, Alabeth Manvers, she thought wryly, you could have been in Charterleigh and safe from all this.

She heard Piers' voice suddenly and turned sharply to see him beckoning to the footman who stood by some velvet drapes. "Will you see that some water is taken to the lady in my box?"

"Very well, Sir Piers." The footman hurried away.

Pausing for a moment, Piers glanced at her, as if debating whether to speak. She thought how much the formality of Court dress suited him, making him look very distinguished, but somehow the disheveled way he wore his hair belied that appearance of correctness. His hand rested lightly on the hilt of his dress sword as at last he approached her, bowing a little stiffly. "Good evening, Lady Alabeth."

"Sir Piers."

"I did not know if it would be wise to address you."

"I am glad that you have, for you give me the opportunity of apologizing to you. You told the truth about the letter and I was in the wrong." Oh, how distant and polite she sounded, and that wasn't how she wished to be at all! But how could she be otherwise when there was no invitation in his manner and when she could not put from her mind the intimacy which he now shared with Adelina?

"I accept your apology, Lady Alabeth, but only on condition that you accept mine."

"Yours?"

"I should not have spoken to you as I did, it was unforgivable."

"I consider the matter to be at an end, sir," she replied, unable to surmount the barriers which seemed to be all around her. His glance was so difficult to read, his manner was cool, and there was Adelina . . . And there was also her own pride, making her conduct herself with dignity when all the time she felt the very opposite.

He inclined his head. "If that is your wish."

"It is."

He withdrew a little. "I think it is time I returned to my box. Good night, Lady Alabeth."

"Good night, Sir Piers."

But as he walked away, it was all she could do not to call out to him. To have done so would have been the height of folly, for it would have invited a snub from which her heart would never have recovered, and so she remained there in silence, watching him until he passed from sight.

Shortly afterward a burst of rapturous applause announced the end of the concert and then the doors were opening as everyone emerged from the boxes. She managed to smile brightly as Charles and Jillian approached.

Jillian was all concern. "Are you well now, Alabeth?"

"I feel better."

"Then you will come on to Ranelagh with us?"

Alabeth's heart sank. "I think not."

"But, Alabeth—"

"I really am not up to Ranelagh, Jillian."

"I would so like to go, for there is to be an orchestra and some dancing."

"Then, of course you must go. Look, there is Octavia, I am sure that she will be going and she will be only too delighted to watch over you." Alabeth hurried across to Octavia, who agreed immediately to look after Jillian.

Charles insisted upon giving Alabeth the use of his carriage, and so she returned to Berkeley Square while he and Jillian joined Octavia's party to go on to Ranelagh.

In the privacy of her own room at last, Alabeth gave in to the tears which had threatened for so long. She cried herself to sleep and knew nothing of the torrential rainstorm which broke over London an hour or so later. At Ranelagh the revelers scattered in great haste, but Jillian and Charles were caught some distance from shelter and Jillian was soon soaked through and shivering. She was still shivering when she arrived home.

20

The following morning Alabeth was roused by Jillian's maid, who was most anxious because her mistress was feverish and seemed not at all well. Alabeth hurried to Jillian's beautiful room, with its delicate Chinese silk on the walls, and found her sister looking indeed far from well. Her cheeks were flushed and her eyes too bright, and when Alabeth learned of the rainstorm at Ranelagh, she knew straightaway that Jillian had taken an ague and the doctor must be sent for.

The doctor too diagnosed an ague and said that Jillian must remain in her bed for at least a week, which precluded them from joining Octavia's house party for Ascot. Jillian was disappointed, but at the same time felt really too ill to be too upset, and the doctor had hardly gone before she had sunk into a restless sleep.

Alabeth immediately sent word to Octavia, who hurried around in great concern, but she accepted that Alabeth had no choice and must remain in Town with Jillian. Charles, on hearing of what had happened, was immediately most anxious, feeling responsible, as he had persuaded Jillian to go to Ranelagh with him, and he was at first disposed to remain in Town too, until Alabeth reasoned with him that there really wasn't anything he could do.

Alabeth was not too disappointed about the enforced stay in London, for it at least gave her time to consider her own position. The week was bound to be quiet, everyone being at Ascot, and she would be able to give a great deal of sensible thought to her feelings for Piers and what she must do about them.

By the end of the week, with Jillian well on the way to recovery, Alabeth had done her thinking and had come to the inevitable conclusion that she must try to forget her love for Piers. She really didn't have any choice, for she had so mishandled everything from the outset that she had ruined any chance she ever had of happiness with him. He now obviously felt nothing for her and indeed had fallen in love instead with Adelina Carver. For Alabeth, acceptance of the truth about herself had come by far too late, and now she must pick up the pieces and continue with her life, with no thought of Piers Castleton at all.

As that week ended, Alabeth had something else to consider too—Count Adam Zaleski. Soon he would be coming each day to the house to give Jillian her tuition, and now that Alabeth knew the true nature of the man, she had no intention whatsoever of exposing either herself or Jillian to his advances. In her heart she knew that the best course would be to cancel the arrangement entirely, but this would have upset Jillian a great deal and might anyway be entirely unnecessary, because the fact that he was disposed to pursue the elder sister did not mean that he was similarly disposed toward the younger. Knowing that he must be guarded against, however, Alabeth announced one morning at breakfast that she had decided it would be best if the lessons were conducted in the presence of a maid. She added hastily that it was certainly not because she did not trust Jillian, but rather that she did not trust the Count, whose reputation was not altogether spotless and who must therefore be regarded as slightly doubtful company for an innocent, unmarried young lady in her first Season in Town. Jillian did not seem to mind the stipulation, and Alabeth felt a great deal better about it—the maid's presence would surely restrict any untoward activities the Count may envisage.

Alabeth was called away to the kitchens shortly afterward, and Jillian sat alone at the table, contemplating the forthcoming lessons—and the Count's rather *risqué* reputation with the ladies. It was inevitable that a man like that would become a little notorious in that direction, for he was quite the most divine of creatures, and his charm and consideration toward Jillian herself could not be faulted. Maybe he was not as immaculate as a Sir Galahad, but he was at least interesting, and above all else, *exciting!* Why couldn't Charles Allister be more like that? Why had he instead to be dull, boring, and tedious?

The hour of the first lesson arrived at last and Jillian was sufficiently recovered to be in readiness. The Count, prompt, was shown into the drawing room. "Good morning, Lady Alabeth. Lady Jillian."

Alabeth nodded coolly. "Sir."

His blue eyes flickered a little at the chill and he smiled instead at Jillian. "I was most concerned to hear of your illness. I trust that you are now fully recovered."

"I am indeed, sir, thank you."

"You look enchanting, as you do always."

Jillian flushed a little, smiling and lowering her eyes. Alabeth reached for the bell which would summon Sanderson. "I know that your time is precious, Count Zaleski, and so we must not delay the commencement of the lesson. Oh, Sanderson, would you see that Lady Jillian's maid goes directly to the music room?"

"Very well, my lady."

Jillian hurried out in a rustle of pale-pink silk, but the Count waited at the door for Alabeth. His glance moved appreciatively over her figure, outlined so beautifully by the soft folds of her leaf-green gown. "I paid a compliment to Lady Jillian on her appearance, but I must also say that I have never seen you look more lovely, Alabeth."

"I asked you before not to address me so familiarly, sir, and must now point out that nothing has changed. You are here to give my sister tuition at the pianoforte, not to pay court to me."

"Why are you so cold? I surely do not deserve to be shut out altogether." His voice was soft, calculated as always to play upon her emotions.

But she was immune to him now. "You do deserve it, sir, as well you know."

Anger flashed into his eyes then, but only briefly before the smile returned to his fine lips. "Perhaps I transgressed a little, but surely I am to be permitted that one mistake? It was, after all, a mistake born purely out of my desire for you. Forgive me, Alabeth, let us forget my sins and begin again."

"My sister is waiting, Count Zaleski."

His smile faltered a little, the set of his jaw looking rather tense, but he seemed gallant enough as he offered his arm and they proceeded up to the music room. She intended to remain there for a short while, for appearance's sake.

He smiled charmingly at Jillian as he entered the room. "Very well, my lady, first of all I will see how you sit at the pianoforte."

She looked surprised. "How I *sit?*"

"But yes, for how can you play your best if you sit incorrectly? Come now, sit as you would normally."

She obeyed.

He pursed his lips, pretending to look a little cross, but with a smile. "That will not do at all, you are far too high."

"But everyone sits like this."

"Everyone does not play well. You look as if you are about to clamber over the top, not play. The fashion for sitting high up in the air is not the best one for a serious musician; it is better to be low, with one's elbows level with the white keys."

He brought another, much lower seat and a moment later Jillian was once again seated. She shifted uncomfortably, looking quite uneasy now.

But he was very gentle and understanding. "Soon you will feel that you have always played from this position, my lady. Now, play something for me, anything you wish."

She selected a sheet of paper and began to play. He listened, his head on one side, nodding now and then, but when she had finished, he was a little stern. "My lady, you play very well indeed, but you use the pedals as if you pump an organ! Take your foot away from them completely, pretend they are not there, and create the tone through the touch of your fingers, thus." He leaned over her, his arms on either side of her as he played several bars. He was so close to her that his sleeve touched her bare arm.

Her lips parted with admiration as he produced a complete range of sound without once having recourse to the pedals. She looked up at him as he finished. "But that was marvelous. I would not have dreamed it possible—"

"Everything is possible with the pianoforte, my lady, as you will soon realize, and to begin with, you must use the metronome." He took the little device down from the shelf.

Jillian was appalled. "But I haven't used one since my first exercises."

"Timing is of the utmost importance; even I use the metronome," he replied firmly, placing it before her and setting it. "Never scorn timing, for if you do, then you will fail."

"I do not wish to fail."

"Then do as I say," he said, smiling down into her big blue eyes.

"Even the metronome?"

"Especially the metronome." He pretended to wag a finger at her.

She laughed. "What shall we begin with?"

"Oh, all the usual things—the Bach fugues, Handel, Scarlatti, Mozart, and so on."

She gasped. *"All* of them?"

"Naturally—and then you will progress to Beethoven."

"It will take a very long time."

"Nonsense, you will skip through them, I promise you. Come now, for after all, time is inmaterial when one wishes to achieve an end." His glance moved toward Alabeth.

It was not of music that he spoke. She gathered her skirts and left the room.

21

Over the next week the house echoed daily to the sound of scales and exercises, and the music room itself became more and more cluttered as Jillian labored her willing way through all the pieces set by the Count. But there was no mistaking that all the hard work was indeed improving her playing, for her fluency became smoother as the week progressed. To her the Count showed only his charming, dashing side, so much so that one morning Jillian had to confess to Alabeth that she found it impossible to believe that such a fine gentleman could ever have cheated at cards. Alabeth, naturally enough, reserved judgment, having witnessed for herself that there was quite another side to Count Adam Zaleski.

He did not seem at all abashed by Alabeth's rebuffs; indeed he lost no opportunity at all of trying to speak to her or to get her on her own, but she managed for the most part to elude him. For Jillian's sake she endured his presence in the house, and that was her only reason for tolerating him, but she had a suspicion that he believed she had embarked upon some elaborate game. She was most careful, therefore, to give him no encouragement whatsoever, being at all times remote and icily civil, for never would she be able to forget how mercilessly he had used her unhappiness to try to seduce her.

Octavia did not return to Town immediately after Ascot, but when she did, her first call was upon Alabeth. Her gray taffeta skirts crackling busily, she crossed the drawing room to kiss Alabeth on the cheek and then sink onto a sofa with a great sigh. "My *dear,* I don't think I can survive much more of this Season, for I swear I am already on my last legs.''

"Oh, I do hope not," remarked Alabeth a little slyly, "for there is Jillian's ball to see to yet.''

"How utterly selfish you are," replied Octavia, smiling. "And how is she? Recovered?''

"Can you not hear?''

The sound of the pianoforte echoed clearly through the house, and Octavia nodded. "How I wish *I* had had the foresight to ask him for private tuition. Just think of all those delicious hours alone with him.''

"I can think of better ways of spending my time.''

Octavia raised a quizzical eyebrow. "Really? You must tell me sometime, for to be sure I must be missing something exciting.''

Alabeth smiled. "Besides, Jillian is most certainly not alone with him. I have seen to it that her maid is in attendance at all times.''

"Perhaps you are wise," Octavia replied, "dull—but wise.'' She listened again as Jillian played a particularly difficult sequence. "She plays like an angel, but then I suppose she is being taught by an arch-angel, is she not?''

"He isn't any sort of angel, he's the very devil," was the short reply.

Octavia was a little taken aback, but she tactfully decided to leave the contentious subject of the Count. "Well, Ascot was a bore," she said at last. "I do not think I have ever enjoyed the week less.''

"Why? What happened?''

"Well, to begin with Charles Allister insisted that we all attend that odious little theater in Windsor to see Mr. Quick perform.''

"The theater is hardly odious, and anyway, you like Mr. Quick.''

"I do indeed, but on this occasion it was virtually impossible to hear a word from the stage.''

"Why?"

"Because, in spite of the Royal Family being present, a group of rather drunken Etonians continually quarreled and interrupted the performance. It was quite disgraceful and they should have been ejected a great deal sooner than they were. By the time the performance continued, I was quite out of sorts with it and wished more than anything else to leave. Piers Castleton had the right idea; he escorted Adelina from the theater the moment the trouble began"

"They were together at Ascot, then?" Alabeth tried to sound only vaguely interested.

"My dear, they were together *everywhere!* It's obviously quite a thing between them. Harry Ponsonby seems to have undergone a complete change of heart, for he's now pursuing her again after having treated her rather poorly before. He'll have a job on his hands, though, for he has a formidable rival in Piers."

"Yes." Alabeth lowered her eyes.

Octavia glanced curiously at her. "Are you feeling quite well?"

"Yes, I'm perfectly all right."

"You look a little peaked. Have you been sleeping?"

"Yes, truly I have, Octavia."

"Well, I think I detect a fibling or two in your replies, for you look far from glowing. I hardly like to ask, but is it perhaps something to do with the Count? A lover's tiff?"

"No, for that would suggest that we have been lovers, which we have not—and which we are never likely to be. He is odious in the extreme and I endure his presence in the house simply and solely because of Jillian. So do not go imagining a liaison which does not exist."

Octavia's shrewd gaze rested thoughtfully on her face for a moment. "Alabeth, I haven't reached this age without knowing a thing or two, and when I look at you, I see someone who is nursing a bruised heart. If it is not the Count, which evidently it is not, then who is it? I swear I haven't detected a sniff of one particular man having carried off your heart—"

Alabeth stood up. "That's because there isn't anyone," she said lightly.

"My dear, I am your friend, your very dearest friend, and it grieves me that you will not confide in me. Perhaps I could help—"

"No one can help."

"Then there is someone?"

"Yes. Now, please, Octavia, I don't wish to—"

"Who is he, Alabeth?"

"I really don't want to say."

"I insist, for I cannot have you looking so utterly miserable, it won't do at all."

Alabeth turned away, knowing that Octavia was far too concerned to have any intention of leaving the subject alone. She took a deep breath and then looked back at Octavia's earnest face. "It's Piers Castleton."

Octavia's eyes widened. "Piers? But you've always loathed him."

"Have I? I think you will find that the truth was very opposite."

"For how long?"

"Too long."

"Before Robert died?"

"Yes."

Octavia was on her feet in a moment, swiftly taking Alabeth's hands. "Oh, my dear, and I've been rattling on so unfeelingly— But you've hidden it all so well, you know, I really believed that you despised him."

Alabeth smiled wryly. "I tried to believe it myself. Anyway, it really doesn't matter now, for Adelina has him, and from all accounts he's very content to be netted."

"Hm. Well, if you ask me, she's most definitely *not* his type. I've said it before and I'll say it again. Alabeth, does Piers know that you—"

"No! At least, maybe he guessed once, but nothing was ever said, and he certainly has no notion of my true feelings for him now. And, Octavia, you are not to tell him, do you hear? If you attempt any of your matchmaking, I will never forgive you."

"But—"

"No, Octavia, I want it to be this way. I have decided that I will get over him, and I will succeed. I've thought of nothing else this past week but how I am going to put this part of my life well and truly behind me, and the last thing I want is for you, no matter how full of good intentions, to meddle."

"But it is hardly meddling," protested Octavia.

"It is, for he is completely indifferent to me, except perhaps to feel decidedly irritated whenever I am near him, and I could not bear it if he learned the truth. Promise me you will say and do nothing, Octavia."

Octavia reluctantly gave in. "Very well, you have my word—for the moment."

"And what does that mean?"

"It means that if sometime in the future I really and truly feel that the circumstances warrant my meddling, as you are pleased to term it, then I will meddle. No, I'm sorry, Alabeth, for it would be very wrong indeed of me to promise once and for all on something as important as this. You obviously love him with all your heart, and you are my dearest friend. I would be a monster indeed if I agreed to stay my hand forever."

"Octavia—"

"Rest assured, my dear, that I will be the soul of discretion, should the occasion ever arise, which it may not. Look at me, my dearest Alabeth, and know that in me you have a sincere and devoted friend. I would never, *never* do anything which would make you unhappy."

Alabeth squeezed the other woman's hands then. "I know," she whispered.

Octavia spoke a little more briskly then. "Now, then, where was I? To be sure I cannot remember. However, here is the matter of the grand regatta at Ranelagh. There was a dreadful mix-up with my invitations and now for the life of me I don't know who received cards and who didn't. Did you and Jillian receive one?"

"No, I'm afraid we didn't."

"Oh, dear, this is very embarrassing. However, I shall issue the invitation personally. Will you both join my party on my barge? It should be so much more agreeable to sit in comfort on cushions and so on, and I can see to it that there is a tidy stock of champagne to add to the delight."

"That does sound exceedingly agreeable and we would both be very pleased to join you. Thank you."

Octavia smiled. "Excellent. Now, I really must fly, for I have a thousand and one things to do and Seaham is being a bear because of all the expense lately. Good-bye for the moment, Alabeth. And Alabeth . . ."

"Yes?"

"I hope you don't regret telling me your secret."

"No, I don't regret it."

Octavia kissed her on the cheek and a moment later was gone. Alabeth sat down again. She felt better for having confided in Octavia, for it was good just to have said aloud that which had been hidden away in her heart for so long. She leaned her head back, listening to Jillian's playing.

"Alabeth?"

Her eyes flew open and she saw the Count in the act of closing the door. "What do you want?" she asked suspiciously, guessing that he had waited until he heard Octavia leaving.

He bowed elegantly before her, looking very debonair and dashing, the epitome of male beauty. "Surely," he murmured, "it is in order for me to discuss Lady Jillian's progress with you?"

"Oh. Why, yes, of course."

"May I sit down?"

"Please do." She indicated a nearby chair, but he sa[t] next to her on the sofa.

"Lady Jillian plays very well, Alabeth; indeed, I woul[d] go so far as to say she is extremely accomplished."

She tried to ignore his persistent use of her first name. "[I] am pleased to hear it," she replied, moving away along th[e] sofa just a little.

"Oh, Alabeth, are you still a little cross with me?"

"I have repeatedly asked you not to address me wit[h] such familiarity," she replied coldly, feeling more an[d] more uneasy as he continued to look at her, a knowin[g] smile playing about his fine lips.

"I did not think I had sinned so very much, Alabeth[,] and now I think you are too cross."

"Please leave me—"

"You are so cross, but it is not with me, is it? You ar[e] cross with yourself, because you know that soon you wi[ll] give in to me."

"How dare you! Get out of here, sir, and do not eve[r] approach me again," she cried, leaping to her feet.

He rose too, and before she knew what was happening[,] he had taken her in his arms and was pressing his lips ove[r] hers. There was an urgency in his kiss, a determination t[o] conquer swiftly, and she struggled furiously, wrenching herself away at last, her eyes bright with anger.

"Leave this house immediately," she breathed. "Ge[t] out before I have you thown out."

His smile began to fade at last. "Have done with thi[s] cat-and-mouse game, Alabeth, for it has gone on long enough."

"It is no game, sirrah. Your attentions are not welcome[,] and they are most certainly refused."

He seized her again, his eyes very dark. "No one spurn[s] me, *no one!*"

Furiously, she tore herself away from him, dealing him a stinging blow on the cheek.

His mouth twisted unpleasantly and his voice shook with ice-cold anger. "You will pay dearly for that—"

"Get out of here!"

"I swear that I will make you regret having played games. Before I have finished, you will wish with all your heart that you had accepted me."

"Will you leave now or shall I send for the servants?"

Without another word he turned on his heels, and she heard his angry steps on the staircase. He called for his hat and gloves, the front door closed, and then she heard his carriage drawing away. Silence descended over the house, broken only by the sound of Jillian's soft playing drifting down from the floor above.

It was some time before Jillian came down and found Alabeth still in the drawing room. "Where is the Count? He said he would only be a few minutes, but now I am told that he has left."

"Yes, he had to go," replied Alabeth, wondering how to explain what had happened.

"Oh."

"He will not come back, Jillian."

Jillian stared at her. "There must be some mistake."

"There is no mistake, he will not be coming back."

"Why?"

"Something he said to me could not be disregarded, and I have forbidden him to return." Alabeth felt decidedly uncomfortable before Jillian's continued gaze.

"Aren't you going to tell me what he said?"

"I would prefer not to. I'm sorry, Jillian, but it really is for the best."

"Have you done this partly because of Charles Allister?"

Alabeth looked up swiftly, a little puzzled. "Why eve do you say that?"

"I thought perhaps Charles had spoken to you."

"I haven't seen him. Why would he speak to me?"

"Because he's jealous of the Count."

"Charles loves you, Jillian."

"I think him more dull than ever and I certainly do no love him."

"I thought you were getting on well."

"I was trying very hard, but I know that I will never lov him. He behaves odiously where the Count is concerne and is most disagreeable."

"I see. Well, I haven't sent the Count away because o Charles, I assure you."

Jillian was a little restless as she went to the window t look out. "I don't think I shall take luncheon today."

"You must eat."

"I'm not particularly hungry, and anyway I will be plie with tea and cakes at Miss Mariner's."

"Are you calling upon her?"

"Didn't I say?" Jillian turned smiling. "Yes, this after noon. Do you mind?"

"No, of course I don't."

"I think I'll do some more practicing."

"You'll wear the pianoforte out."

"The Count says that the more you play, the more th pianoforte lives."

"That does sound like something he would say."

Jillian went out and a few minutes later Alabeth heard her playing. She chose a piece she had learned during the past week from the Count. It was a Polish love song, ful of poignancy and dark fire, but Alabeth did not really notice, for she was preoccupied with her own thoughts.

22

Before the grand regatta at Ranelagh Gardens, they had one other important engagement: a masquerade at Minsterworth House, the Piccadilly residence of the Earl and Countess of Minsterworth. The Countess was known to be miffed at being upstaged by nearly every other hostess of note when it came to engaging Count Zaleski to play for her guests, but he was still the lion of the Season and much feted, so the Countess took a little solace from this. She decided to make up for having come a little too late on the scene by providing exquisite decorations and a positive ocean of champagne. The lights of Minsterworth House could be seen from a considerable distance and the crush of elegant carriages and chairs in Piccadilly threatened to bring that thoroughfare to a complete standstill.

Alabeth went reluctantly to the masquerade, for her spirits were very low indeed as rumor made it more and more clear that the liaison between Piers and Adelina was serious. It was now being said that London's first courtesan was to make a match of it with London's first Corinthian, and Adelina seemed to be going out of her way to make certain the rumors proliferated.

In order to conceal completely how unhappy she really was, Alabeth chose to wear yellow for the masquerade, wishing to appear lighthearted and carefree and knowing that yellow helped a great deal to give this effect. Safe behind her mask, she forced herself to enter thoroughly into the spirit of things, dancing every dance and generally exuding an air of jaunty happiness which defied anyone to wonder if the opposite was perhaps closer to the truth. The

pain she felt at the cool, barely perceptible acknowledgment she received from Piers was concealed completely by
the dazzling smile she bestowed upon a gentleman who at
that moment asked her if she would partner him for the
ländler. Not by so much as a flicker did she reveal the hurt
she endured throughout the evening, for she kept
reminding herself of how she appeared to others in her
sunshine yellow, the flowers in her red hair and the pearls
at her throat—she *looked* radiant, and that was the role
she acted to perfection from the moment she entered Minsterworth House until the moment she left it again before
dawn. No one, least of all Piers Castleton, knew that Lady
Alabeth Manvers was weeping inside.

Jillian, on the other hand, was as happy as she appeared.
She wore old-rose silk and had begged Alabeth's rubies to
go with it. Her hair glittered with tiny diamonds, and her
eyes, behind her little black mask, shone with excitement.
Indeed, she seemed infused with so much *joie de vivre* that
Alabeth was almost concerned, for such sparkle coupled
with a noticeable lack of appetite suggested that Lady
Jillian Carstairs was most definitely in love—but that
could not be so, for there did not seem to be any one
particular *beau* upon whom she bestowed her favor. Poor
Charles was most definitely not the recipient of any favor,
for with him Jillian was once again cool and offhand, not
quite having reverted to her former aversion for him, but
almost. It was a little sad, for Alabeth would have sworn at
one time that Jillian had indeed begun to like him a great
deal more. Alabeth smiled a little wryly, as it had
obviously been an illusion, born of Jillian's ability to be as
consummate an actress as her elder sister was now showing
herself to be.

Charles was inconsolable, refusing Octavia's efforts to
make him smile and declining any thought of dancing. He
sat on a sofa, watching Jillian as she smiled and danced,
and his misery was almost palpable as she leaned a little

closer to one particularly handsome young Hussar officer.

Alabeth had complete sympathy with how he was feeling, for was she not enduring the same? Each time Piers smiled down into Adelina's eyes, each time his hand touched hers, everything which passed between them, cut through Alabeth like a knife. But she laughed, and smiled, and danced gaily through the evening and into the early hours of the night, and the tears did not gleam in her eyes once.

In spite of the fact that the Count had played a great number of times before what amounted to the same audience, the moment of his appearance was still greeted with great delight, everyone moving forward in order to secure as advantageous a place as possible for the recital. Alabeth held back, not having any wish at all to be close to him, but Jillian managed to secure a place directly by the pianoforte, thus ensuring a further lowering of Charles Allister's already sunken spirits.

Count Zaleski looked as refined and elegant as ever when he took his seat at the pianoforte, and there was no sign now of the ugly fury which had twisted his face when he had last spoken to Alabeth. He wove his breathless spell over his audience, his genius effortless and his mastery complete, and on his face was a look of melancholy which went perfectly with the sad music he played, creating havoc in the tender hearts of the ladies who gazed so adoringly at him. Alabeth was immune to him now; she felt nothing but dislike as she watched him, and only once did his glance stray toward her, lingering malevolently for a moment before moving on. A smile played around his lips as he looked instead at Jillian, whose rapt expression was so admiring.

Charles had managed to find a place fairly close to Jillian and had attempted to persuade her to leave her prominent place and sit with him, but she had refused with a most definite toss of her golden curls. Now, however, she could not help glancing at her unhappy suitor, her expression taunting him that, no matter what *he* thought, *she* knew the Count to be an angel and much misunderstood. Alabeth sighed, for it was evident that Jillian was not prepared at any price to believe ill of the Count, whether it was Charles telling her the Pole cheated at cards or Alabeth herself telling her that he behaved dishonorably. To Jillian, Count Adam Zaleski was the personification of romance and therefore everything about him was to be praised.

The Count's magnificent music echoed poignantly over the glittering chamber, and Alabeth turned her head a little to look at Piers as he stood by Adelina's chair. He had removed his mask and she was able to see his face quite clearly. His expression was thoughtful and a little cool as he watched the Count, and then, as if he sensed she was watching him, he looked directly at her, the diamond pin flashing in his neckcloth as he turned. His glance was distant and he neither smiled nor inclined his head before looking away again. The act was calculated and could not be mistaken, and she felt as if he had publicly struck her. She needed every last ounce of willpower not to bow her head and give in to the hot tears which were suddenly so close, but she trembled a little as she forced herself to look casually away from him, for all the world as if she neither knew of the snub nor cared.

The music came to an end and Jillian was the first to rise to her feet, clapping ecstatically, and Alabeth saw that it was being remarked how much favor the Earl of Wallborough's younger daughter was showing to the handsome Pole. Several raised fans were evidence that not only was this being thought, it was being said too. Alabeth's heart sank. Oh, Jillian, *please* be a little more discreet and a little more restrained. . . .

Charles appeared at Alabeth's side. "The fellow can do no wrong, it seems," he said bitterly.

"It would appear that you are right."

"Why can't she see him for what he is—a transparent blackguard!"

"Hush, Charles, for you may be overheard."

"I swear that I don't care if I am," he declared, "for I have endured too much tonight."

"Please, Charles—" Alabeth was a little uneasy, for he was obviously much goaded.

In reply, he suddenly drew her hand through his arm and began to walk resolutely toward the pianoforte, where Jillian was in animated conversation with the Count, who was being flatteringly attentive toward his former pupil.

Alabeth was alarmed, but thought it better to perhaps go along with him rather than make a scene by refusing. Besides, it was hardly likely that Charles would really provoke anything untoward.

The Count watched their approach a little warily, especially as he could tell that Alabeth was uncertain about her escort. Jillian's fan began to move more swiftly as she too perceived the anger and determination in Charles' eyes, and she looked nervously at Alabeth.

Charles bowed before the Count, flicking a lace-edged handkerchief over a spotless black sleeve for a moment before speaking. "You played well, sir, I congratulate you."

"Thank you."

"It seems to be my lot today to heap praise upon the efforts of Frenchmen."

"With all due respect, sir, I am not a Frenchman." The Count's blue eyes were very guarded now.

"No? Why, damn me if I hadn't forgotten you were Polish. Still, you're as much a Frenchman as makes no difference now, eh?"

"As you wish, sir, I do not intend to make an issue of it." This was said entirely for Jillilan's benefit and he was rewarded by the look of approval in her eyes.

"Issue?" replied Charles. "Why, no, sir, of course not, for why would one wish to make an issue of so trivial a matter? As I was saying, it seems to be my lot today to pay compliments to Frenchmen."

"And how is that?"

"I simply had to take myself along to that newspaper fellow, I forget his name for the moment, but he publishes a most informative paper called *L'Ambigu*. Oh, yes, I recall his name now—Peltier, Jean Peltier." This last was said loud enough to attract a little attention and a number of people looked swiftly at the small group by the piano-forte, as well they might look, for Jean Peltier was an extreme supporter of the Bourbons and *L'Ambigu* frequently published outrageous criticisms of First Consul Bonaparte. It had also seen fit recently to cast aspersions upon the Count's genius, questioning his talent and likening the sounds he produced to that of a herd of cows crossing a wooden bridge.

Alabeth held her breath with sharp dismay at this, and Jillian's eyes widened with amazement that anyone could deliberately set about provoking an argument which must surely end in a challenge.

The Count stiffened with quivering anger. "Sir," he breathed, "I think it vulgar and of extremely poor taste that you should praise this man who spreads such calumny about the First Consul and indeed about myself."

"Calumny? Why, I thought he had put a sure finger on the pulse of truth, sir. Indeed, so exact and in accordance with my own views are his comments that I do not think I could have put it better myself." Charles' handkerchief continued to flick slowly.

Alabeth tugged on his sleeve. "Please, Charles, have done with this immediately."

"Alabeth is right, Charles," interrupted a new voice, "for I think you've made your point now." It was Piers, stepping firmly between Charles and the Count.

"Made it?" Charles cried. "I haven't even begun."

"You've said all you're going to say," Piers replied softly, "for I am telling you that you have. Don't be foolish now, for it will do no good and may do a great deal of harm to proceed." His voice was reasonable, but his eyes told Charles that he had no intention whatsoever of letting him utter one more unwise word.

Charles hesitated, but then nodded. "Very well," he said, to the inexpressible relief of both Alabeth and Jillian, "I will say no more."

The Count stepped angrily forward, and his voice fell on a completely hushed gathering, for even the orchestra had stopped playing now. "You *will* say more, sir, for you will apologize for what you have said."

Slowly, Piers turned to eye him. "And you, sir, will then have to apologize to me for having been ill-bred enough to continue making a scene when I have done my utmost to pour oil on these particular troubled waters." He smiled faintly.

For a moment it seemed that the Count might proceed in spite of this, but then he thought better of it, turning angrily on his heel and walking from the chamber. There was a great deal of whispering as Jillian made as if she would follow him, but then Piers restrained her by very firmly catching hold of her hand. "No, my lady, I think you must remain here," he said in a low voice, "for to pursue him now would be to provoke even more comment than you have already caused."

Her cheeks flushed angrily. "You have no right—"

"I have every right, having taken it upon myself yet again to see that there is more decorum and common sense than shown hitherto. As for you, Charles, I begin to tire of forever intervening to keep you from the point of an opponent's sword, and I trust that from now on you will act with more restraint. Now, then, you and Lady Jillian here will toddle obediently onto the floor and dance a nice, elegant minuet, you will observe every last detail of etiquette, and you will allow the Countess's masquerade to proceed in a proper manner."

Charles had the grace to look a little ashamed of himself, but defiance flashed brightly in Jillian's eyes. Alabeth looked sternly at her. "Do as you are told, Jillian."

Reluctantly, Jillian took the hand Charles held out to her, and a moment later they had joined the other couples on the floor as the first strains of a minuet began to play.

Piers turned to Alabeth, his gray eyes shrewd. "It is strange, is it not, how different people react in different ways to the same emotion?"

"Emotion? I don't understand."

"Jealousy." Smiling, he bowed and left her.

23

The following morning Alabeth took the first opportunity of pointing out to Jillian that she had not conducted herself all that gracefully at the masquerade. She worded herself very carefully, not wishing to offend or run the risk of a return to their former feuding, and Jillian agreed that perhaps she had been a little unwise. She apologized for having shown favor to the Count when she knew he had behaved insultingly toward Alabeth, but she confessed that she had always found him to be the perfect gentleman and was therefore adhering to the time-honored maxim: speak as you find. In all honesty Alabeth could not find this blameworthy, for although she herself knew the Count to be a toad of the first order, it was hardly to be expected that Jillian would know the truth of that, especially if he was putting himself out to be more than a little charming. They therefore agreed to disagree about the Count.

About Jillian's conduct toward Charles Allister, however, Alabeth could not find anything with which to really exonerate Jillian. If Charles was an unwanted and unwelcome suitor, then she should have told him so a little more discreetly and thus spared him the odiousness of the previous evening, for it was Jillian's behavior which had so provoked him and caused the unpleasant scene with the Count. That did not, of course, excuse Charles, but it was only right that Jillian should accept her share of the blame. Jillian was not as amenable about this as she had been about the Count, for she grumbled that Charles was dull and tiresome and that he thoroughly irritated her. However, when Alabeth asked her to write a polite and elegantly phrased letter to him, informing him that she was declining his suit, Jillian refused, saying that there was surely no need at all to write such a letter. Alabeth persisted for a while but then gave up, for it was hardly possible to stand over Jillian watching each word being written, and if Jillian was quite determined not to write, then the whole exercise became pointless. They agreed to disagree about Charles too.

They parted a little later, Alabeth to call upon Aunt Silchester and Jillian to once again visit Miss Mariner. Alabeth wondered what on earth two souls as diverse as her sister and the rather prim, elderly spinster could find to talk about on successive days, but Jillian merely said that they found each other's company most congenial. Alabeth could not help thinking that if Jillian could complain that Charles Allister was dull company, then Miss Mariner must be driving her up the wall with boredom.

Alabeth walked to her appointment with Aunt Silchester. She viewed the prospect with even less enthusiasm than before, for surely word would have reached the nosy old biddy about what had happened at the masquerade, and there would be a fine old wigging waiting in Baswick Street for so lax and ineffectual a chaperone as Alabeth must appear to be. However, Dame Fortune was smiling on her for once, for the story had by some miracle failed to reach her aunt, and so the visit was passed in an almost agreeable way discussing the arrangements for Jillian's ball. Aunt Silchester was prepared to discuss this at length, and this was solely because of Octavia's involvement. Being a Duchess, Octavia was deemed to be most suitable and quite worthy of favor from one who had married into the exalted Silchesters. Alabeth escaped back to Berkeley Square at last, feeling that she had done her duty for the time being and would not need to run the gauntlet of Baswick Street again for a while.

Jillian returned rather late from calling on Miss

Mariner, causing luncheon to be delayed somewhat and then making Alabeth a little anxious by announcing that she really didn't feel very hungry. Alabeth found Jillian's mood of bubbling excitement a little disturbing, for once again she was exuding that air which one always associates with the first dizzy flush of a new love. Tentative questions however, drew only a blank. Jillian picked at her salad and then fled up to the music room to practice once again at the pianoforte. She played the same Polish love song over and over again until Alabeth felt like screaming if it did not stop.

Lord Gainsford's unexpected arrival at the house later in the afternoon was greeted by Alabeth with undisguised relief, and she agreed with great delight to drive out with him in his new curricle. An hour in the fresh air of Hyde Park made her feel a great deal better, especially when that hour was spent in the company of such a fine old gentleman, and she returned to the house having managed to set aside all thought of the perplexing problems which seemed to be besetting her own private life and which continually surrounded anything to do with her sister.

They had not retired to bed until four in the morning after the masquerade, and Alabeth was determined that they should both go to bed early that night, especially as the next day was the day of the grand regatta and the fireworks display, which would not even commence until well after midnight. They spent a quiet evening together, although Jillian was in a restless mood, and they went up to their respective rooms at half-past ten. Alabeth seemed to have hardly laid her head on the pillow before she was fast asleep.

The bedroom was filled with moonlight as the clock on the mantelpiece chimed two. Alabeth had requested her maid to leave the window open as the room had been a little close and stuffy, but now a fresh breeze had sprung up from nowhere, billowing the heavy lace curtains and

knocking a tortoiseshell comb from the dressing table to
the highly polished floor below. It fell with a clatter and
Alabeth sat up with a start, pushing her hair back from her
face and looking around to see what had happened. The
breeze was cool as it touched her warm skin and she
shivered a little, slipping from the bed to close the window,
but what she saw in the garden below made her halt in
astonishment—and then dismay.

Jillian was walking toward the house from the direction
of the mews lane. She was dressed in a mauve silk chemise
gown, her hair was intricately looped with strings of
pearls, and her expensive cashmere shawl dragged on the
path behind her. She walked slowly, pausing now and then
to raise her hem a little and practice some dance steps, for
all the world as if she had but a moment before been taught
them. Which, from her appearance, she probably had!

Alabeth felt the stirrings of anger as she watched, for
Jillian had quite obviously been out somewhere—but
where? And who with? There had not been any invitations
for tonight and Jillian had certainly not mentioned any
unexpected appointment; indeed, when she had gone to
her room earlier, she had most definitely given the impression that she too was intending to go straight to bed.
And yet here she was, dressed up to the nines and returning
from some unknown engagement—and without even a
maid as chaperone. Picking up her own shawl, Alabeth
hurried from the room, determined to confront her sister
immediately and trusting that some sort of satisfactory
explanation would be forthcoming for this flagrant breach
of the rules.

She waited on the staircase, listening as Jillian's light
steps approached from the rear of the house. Jillian was
humming and was quite obviously in excellent spirits. She
reached the cool green vestibule and then paused again,
lifting her hem to practice the dance steps.

"And where, pray, you have been?" inquired Alabeth coldly.

With a gasp, Jillian whirled about. "Alabeth! You startled me!"

"As you startled me a moment ago when I looked from my window and saw you."

Jillian's eyes were wary. "Saw me? Doing what?"

"Walking back from the mews lane after attending some engagement I know nothing of."

The blue eyes cleared. "Oh, Alabeth, you don't really believe I would do that, do you?"

"What else am I to believe when I see you dressed like that?"

"I *was* in the garden, I do not deny that, but I was only walking in the cool air. I had another of my headaches—"

"And you paused to don evening togs before slipping out?"

"No. Oh, it sounds so silly—"

"Allow me to be the judge of that."

"Well, I couldn't sleep and so I decided to try on various gowns and see which one I would wear for the regatta. By the time I had tried this one on and my maid had finished looping the pearls through my hair, I felt quite hot and bothered, and so I simply decided to stroll for a while in the moonlight." She smiled, her eyes very wide and innocent, and Alabeth did not quite know what to say. It was an explanation, such an unexpectedly ordinary one that it had the trappings of truth about it, and yet Jillian simply had not looked as if she had been taking an idle stroll, she had looked as if she had been returning to the house after alighting from a carriage in the mews lane.

Jillian came reproachfully to the foot of the staircase. "Alabeth, you don't really think I'd go out like that without telling you, do you?"

"You are quite capable of doing so," Alabeth reminded her.

"That was then; I couldn't possibly do it now. Please Alabeth, you must believe me."

"You *are* being honest with me, aren't you? I mean you've been in such a strange mood just recently—" There seemed no point in beating about the bush. "Jillian, have you been seeing someone? A *beau?*"

"A *beau?*" Jillian giggled a little. "Of course I haven't You'd know about it, wouldn't you? There isn't anyone truly there isn't. I'm just like I am because I'm enjoying myself so much—it really is quite marvelous to be courted by so many handsome young lords and to know that any one of them might soon be my husband."

She sounded so very convincing, so plausible, that Alabeth felt she had no option but to accept the explanation. And yet, there was something about the way Jillian was avoiding her eyes which was so strongly reminiscent of their father that Alabeth could not overlook it. As they went up the stairs together, Alabeth knew that she wasn't satisfied with what she'd been told, that at the very least she'd have to make discreet inquiries of Sanderson to find out if one of the carriages had been ordered. She felt sneaky and disloyal, but Jillian was her responsibility and it was hardly wise to take any chances when her sister could once again be launching herself into an unwise affair of the heart. Jillian might mean well, but she was prey to her own weaknesses, not the least of which was this constant and urgent quest for true romantic love. It would perhaps not have been so bad had she not bestowed an undeserved rosy glow upon certain unworthy gentlemen.

After a restless night spent mulling over all the dreadful possibilities about which gentleman might possibly be involved, Alabeth waited the next morning until Jillian had gone out shopping before summoning Sanderson to the

rawing room and asking him to make *very* discreet in-
uiries of the grooms and coachman regarding the
revious evening. He returned a little later, telling her that
one of the carriages had been requested and certainly
one of them had left the coach house. She felt a little
ore easy in her mind after this, but somehow the doubt
ill niggled away.

Jillian returned from shopping complaining of a head-
che; indeed, she said the pain was so bad that she would
ave to take some primrose tea and retire to her bed for a
hile. The hour approached when they would have to
ave for the regatta at Ranelagh, but Jillian remained in
er bed, sending her maid to tell Alabeth that she would
ave to go alone to the regatta as the headache showed no
gns of going away and was really too bad for the noise
nd excitement of the regatta to be contemplated.

Alabeth hurried to Jillian's room, finding it in semi-
arkness, the curtains drawn tightly against the sun, which
as trying to stream in from the clear heavens. The floral
lk hangings of the bed were also drawn, and Jillian lay
urled up between the lavender-scented sheets, her face
ale beneath the floppy frills of her night bonnet.

"Oh, Jillian, I do not like to go without you," began
labeth anxiously.

"I shall be all right once I have managed to sleep."

"It doesn't seem right to leave you."

"But you've given your word to Octavia," replied
illian quickly, "and why should you forego the delights of
e regatta simply because I am a little indisposed. Please
o, Alabeth, for I shall feel totally wretched if you don't."

"If you're certain—"

"Of course I am." Jillian squeezed Alabeth's hand reas-
uringly and smiled.

"All right." Alabeth bent to kiss the pale cheek and
hen returned to her own room to begin dressing for the

regatta, where she would be bound to see Piers wit
Adelina and where she would therefore be made ver
miserable. She chose to wear yellow again.

24

She set off in the landau, her yellow gown and golden spencer indeed managing to make her look as sunny as the day itself. She also wore a gypsy bonnet, tied on with wide yellow satin ribbon, and over it was draped a little veil to protect her back from the heat, which would be all the more fierce on the Thames. The landau drove smartly toward Chelsea, conveying her to a social occasion which under normal circumstances would have promised a great deal of enjoyment, but which today offered little such prospect.

She had not proceeded far when suddenly the carriage began to travel much more slowly, and at last came to a standstill on a tree-lined avenue. The coachman climbed down and she leaned out. "What is it?"

"I believe one of the horses has gone lame, my lady."

"Oh, no."

He inspected the nearside lead horse and then came to speak to her. "He is lame, my lady, and I think I should take him back to the mews and bring another."

"Very well."

He began to unharness the horse and she alighted from the carriage, shaking out her skirts and glancing up at the flawless blue through the dappled branches of the trees. How magnificent a day it was, quite perfect for a regatta.

She heard the other carriage approaching but did not at first give it much thought. It wasn't until she realized that it was halting that she turned to look at it, recognizing it at once: it belonged to Piers Castleton.

Piers alighted. He was alone. He looked very elegant in a

189

wine-red coat and pale-gray breeches, and his dark curls shone in the sunlight as he removed his tall hat and approached her. "Good afternoon, Alabeth. Do you have some trouble?"

"One of the horses is lame."

"Are you bound for the regatta?"

"Yes."

"Then please allow me to convey you there, as that is my destination as well."

"There is no need—" she began.

"For me to concern myself?" He gave a faint smile.

"No need for you to put yourself out, sir," she finished.

"I see. Well, I am and ever will be a gentleman, my lady, and nothing would permit me to drive past and not offer you my assistance. Please accept a place in my carriage and thus allow me to carry out my gentlemanly obligation." He smiled a little wryly.

"If you are sure—"

"I am."

"Then I accept. Thank you."

Her gloved hand shook just a little as she took the arm he offered, and he instructed her coachman to go back carefully to Berkeley Square. She sat back on the magnificent upholstery of his carriage and a moment later the perfectly matched grays were straining forward, their hooves striking sparks from the cobbles.

He lounged opposite her, one gleaming Hessian boot resting on the seat beside her. The countless things she wished to say to him hung trembling on her lips, but she couldn't say one of them, for it was as if Adelina were present in the carriage.

He spoke first. "Yellow becomes you well, Alabeth. You should wear it more often."

"Thank you."

"It is such a cheerful shade, is it not?"

She felt almost as if he knew exactly why she had chosen the color and she shifted her position a little uncomfortably, determined to change the subject. "Will Lady Adelina be with you at Ranelagh?"

"I believe so."

"H-how is she?"

"In excellent spirits."

"Oh."

"She is also extremely triumphant and most pleased with her scheming."

"I beg your pardon?"

He smiled a little. "It doesn't matter."

A few more minutes of silence passed and then he spoke again. "Why is Lady Jillian not with you?"

"She is indisposed."

"Does that mean you've ensured her good behavior by locking her in her room?"

She flushed. "It means that she has a headache."

"Ah. Well, to be sure, I could not have blamed you had you turned jailer."

"She is very young."

"Are you so very old, then?"

She looked away.

"My poor Alabeth, you have had a time of it recently, haven't you?" he murmured. "Prised out of your Kent sanctuary, thrust into the hurly-burly of one of the most important Seasons in years, forced to endure a dreadful variety of problems and pitfalls, only some of which are of your own making, and all the time having to wear a new cloak which doesn't sit well on your pretty shoulders."

"If by cloak you mean my having charge of my sister—"

"That is only a fraction of what I speak."

"I don't really wish to discuss it," she said, her flush becoming hotter.

"No, I didn't for one moment think you would," he remarked dryly, glancing out as the carriage entered Chelsea.

She was relieved when they reached Ranelagh Gardens and he helped her to alight. He held her hand for a moment, looking down into her green eyes, and she thought he was going to say something to her, but instead he released her.

"Enjoy the regatta, Alabeth."

"I trust that I will, as I trust you will, sir. Thank you for your kindness in offering me a place in your carriage."

"Think nothing of it, Lady Alabeth." His gray eyes seemed to be laughing at her in the moment before she turned and hurried away from him.

The gardens of Ranelagh House had been popular with the fashionable world since they had opened sixty years before. They were no longer exclusive and therefore not the frequent haunt of the *beau monde*, but for certain gala occasions such as this regatta, they were splendid still. The centerpiece of the gardens was the building known as the Rotunda, with its four great portals like triumphal arches. Built entirely of wood, it was a vast amphitheater meant to resemble the Roman Pantheon, and it was the scene of many a fine concert, indeed the infant prodigy Mozart had played there at the age of only eight and a half. All around the Rotunda lay the gardens themselves, very elegant and inviting and containing many hidden arbors where at night secret assignations could be kept without fear of discovery. There was a shrine to the god Pan, a Venetian temple built across the pretty canal, and everywhere there were fountains, flowering shrubs and trees, and the hundreds of colored lanterns which at night gave the gardens their particular magic and excitement.

Alabeth hurried toward the part of the Embankment where the Duke and Duchess of Seaham's splendid golden barge was moored, and as she emerged at the edge of the water, she saw that the whole river was covered with pleasure vessels and she overheard someone say that the gathering stretched from London Bridge to the Ship Tavern at Millbank. Flotillas of small craft bobbed on the glittering water as the great pageant of the regatta spread out before the elegant crowd thonging the shore.

The Seaham barge was moored to a small quay, its gangplank painted gold and tied with countless ribbons in the Seaham colors. Octavia reclined alone on a red-and-gold-striped couch which bore more than an accidental likeness to Cleopatra's divan. The flimsy, rather transparent gown she wore was also strongly reminiscent of ancient Egypt, as was her hair, worn *à l'Egyptienne;* she had even got up her long-suffering page as a slave, and he stood miserably behind her, wafting a huge ostrich fan to and fro. There was a silken canopy over the couch and it fluttered a little in the light sea breeze, the effect of the Nile would have been complete, had it not been for the Thames language of an exasperated bargeman who was shaking his furious fist at another.

Octavia waved a gracious hand as Alabeth came aboard. "Welcome, oh, faithful subject—and mind my asp." A covered basket was hastily whisked from the chair which Alabeth had chosen.

Alabeth laughed. "It would not do to extinguish the asp before you require it, would it?"

"Hardly."

"And where is Caesar?"

"Sulking at home in Rome because I am too extravagant."

"And so you are."

"Wretch, you are supposed to uphold me, not criticize! And while inquiries concerning missing persons are the order of the day—where is Jillian?"

"Also languishing at home, but nursing a headache."

"Oh, dear. Still, her absence does give me the opportunity of telling you a tiny whisper I've heard."

"Whisper?"

"About Jillian."

"Oh, no."

"It may be nothing, for I heard it from someone whose indulgence in scandal-mongering is quite notorious, but on the other hand I think it only right that I should tell you. It seems that late last night—very late—Jillian was seen alone in a carriage with a gentleman, and their manner together was described to me as intimate."

Alabeth stared at her, seeing again quite clearly Jillian's mauve-clad figure coming back up the garden.

Octavia leaned across to put a hand on Alabeth's. "Forgive me for saying anything, but I did think you should know. *Was* Jillian out last night?"

Alabeth took a long breath. "I don't really know." She explained what had happened.

Octavia pursed her lips. "It don't look good, and that's a fact."

"What am I to do, Octavia?"

"Have it out with her the moment you return to the house."

"She will not be well pleased."

"Are you well pleased at being told scandalous rumors about her?"

"No, but—"

"But nothing, she'll have to put up with it. I find her a most vexing creature, for although I love her dearly, she can be the most exasperating and idiotic of young ladies. Dizzy, that's the word for her, quite dizzy."

"I wish I was back in Charterleigh," said Alabeth miserably.

Octavia grinned. "Oh, I rather think I'd like a sovereign for every time you've thought *that* recently."

"You'd be even more disgustingly rich than you already are."

"Yes, I know. Come now, let's think of more pleasing things—like this wondrous regatta, for unless it begins soon I fancy the weather will wash it away."

"But the sun is shining and the sky is quite blue," Alabeth protested. "There isn't even much of a breeze."

"It's going to change very shortly—or so I'm reliably informed by my bargeman. He feels it in his— Well, I won't tell you where he feels it, but suffice it that he and the other bargemen sense there to be a fine old summer storm on the way."

"I don't believe it."

"I do, for if Old Jarge says there is, then there is." Octavia nodded in the direction of a particularly weather-beaten bargeman, seated grumpily near the prow carefully cleaning his clay pipe.

Alabeth looked at him and then inevitably looked beyond him at a small pleasure craft which was being rowed out onto the river. Piers lounged on the cushions in the stern and Adelina was beside him, her full lips rosy red as she smiled beguilingly up into his eyes. On a nearby vessel Alabeth also saw Harry Ponsonby, his handsome face as stormy as the weather Old Jarge was so confidently forecasting.

"Oh, dear," murmured Octavia, also watching the scene. "I suppose that puts the lid on your enjoyment of the day."

"I came here knowing what to expect."

"I'd tell you to forget him, if I didn't know from experience how fatuous advice like that can sound at times. Still, cheer up a little, for at least you are to be spared the odious Count and his wretched pianoforte today."

"I am?"

"I am reliably informed—"

"By Old Jarge again?"

"Hardly, my dear, he don't have access to Court!" chided Octavia good-humoredly. "As I was saying, I am reliably informed that the dear Count won't be here as he's to play for Their Majesties this evening."

"Would it be a dreadful pun to say that you appear to have changed your tune about him?"

"It would, but I will excuse you. Of *course* I've changed my tune about the wretched fellow, for after what you told me of him at the masquerade, I doubt that I'll ever be able to say a civil word to him again. He was odious to you and that puts him most firmly beyond the pale as far as I'm concerned. He may be the lion of the Season, but he's proved himself to be a shameless alley cat."

Alabeth smiled fondly at her. "Oh, Octavia, you are surely the finest friend anyone ever had."

"I know," replied Octavia infuriatingly, and then she glanced up as a breath of unexpected wind swept across the barge. "You see, Old Jarge was right, there's a different feel to the air, don't you agree?"

Alabeth looked across the water, which was not as smooth and shining as it had been, for the breeze was rippling the surface. The canopy overhead stirred and the yellow ribbons on her bonnet fluttered prettily.

Octavia was pensive. "Old Jarge is always right; he was right all those years ago too."

"Right about what?"

"About the mistake I was making marrying Seaham." Octavia grinned. "I've learned to pay attention since then, as becomes a mere Duchess when being advised by wise old retainers."

Dusk was falling as the flotillas of boats and barges returned at last to the shore, having witnessed an excellent afternoon and evening of racing, although toward the end the weather had begun to interfere, making the water choppy and rowing difficult. The wind had continued to rise and clouds had begun to scud across the sky, although as the sun set it was still very pleasant and no one felt deterred.

The Seaham barge was moored to its quay and Octavia and her guests stepped ashore, intent now upon adjourning to the Rotunda for the feast and the fireworks display, which would take place much later. Octavia was in high spirits, having satisfied her desire to gamble by placing a number of successful wagers, and now the prospect of something good to eat was most inviting.

Alabeth was not in such high spirits, having endured an afternoon throughout which she had been afforded a view of Piers and Adelina together in their boat. They walked ahead of her now, making their way through the illuminated gardens, where a hidden orchestra was playing, toward the Rotunda, which was already echoing with the noise and chatter of the elegant guests.

The interior of the wooden building was made bright by thousands of candles protected by glass cases and by immense chandeliers suspended from the ceiling far above. There were scarlet and gold hangings festooned everywhere, and baskets of sweet-smelling flowers, and another orchestra was playing music on a raised stand to one side. The walls were lined with private boxes where the guests could take refreshment in some degree of privacy, and Octavia and her party repaired immediately to theirs and were served with ice-cold champagne and succulent cold-chicken salads.

Octavia looked impatiently around. "Where's Charles? He told me that he would be here in time to eat and yet he isn't. Ah, I do believe I see him now. Charles? We're over here!" Her raised voice echoed over the clamor all around, and Charles turned immediately, the smile on his lips fading when he saw that Jillian was not present.

Octavia patted the seat next to her. "I'll have to do instead, m'boy."

He took his place dutifully, glancing at Alabeth. "Where is she?"

"She has a headache and didn't come."

"Oh, well, at least I know she isn't with that prinked music-master!"

"That's quite enough of that, Charles," reproved Octavia. "You said your piece at the masquerade and we don't want to hear it again, no matter how strongly you feel. Come now, eat up your chicken like a good boy and be agreeable."

"Very well, I'll be agreeable and tell you a piece of news I have just this moment heard."

"What news? Is it scandalous?" Octavia was all interest.

"Scandalous? Well, I don't know. I do know I find it surprising, in spite of all that's gone on recently."

"Don't be infuriating and get on with it," said Octavia impatiently.

"I have it on good authority that Piers Castleton has asked Adelina Carver to marry him."

Octavia stared at him and a murmur of interest went around the nearby guests. Alabeth lowered her eyes to the plate of salad, seeing it in only a blur.

Charles looked well pleased with the stir he had caused. "You see what I mean? Everyone has known of their association and yet no one really thought it would end in him making a marriage offer."

Octavia's eyes fled momentarily to Alabeth and then back to Charles. "And who is this reliable authority who told you?"

"Why, Adelina herself. I was talking with Harry Ponsonby a moment ago when she came over to us. Harry was most put out; he stormed away without another word."

Octavia was thoughtful. "And did Adelina tell you if she had accepted Piers proposal?"

"Eh? Oh, I don't know, I was so astounded at Harry's conduct that I didn't think of asking her."

Alabeth found this latest thing the last straw, and she folded her napkin and rose to her feet, looking apologetically at Octavia. "Forgive me."

"I quite understand, my dear."

Charles got up too, looking a little alarmed. "I say, I haven't said something wrong, have I?"

Alabeth smiled. "No, Charles, it's nothing to do with you."

"Well, maybe I can escort you to your carriage, for I can't say I find it as interesting when a certain person is not present." He smiled in return.

She had almost forgotten that she had no carriage. "Oh, my carriage—Charles, can you take me home?"

"With pleasure."

The wind had risen still more as she and Charles left the Rotunda to cross the shadowy gardens where the leaves rustled and the lanterns swayed. On the river the masts undulated and rigging flapped noisily as the gathering storm swept inland from the distant sea. The promised gale was almost upon them and Charles glanced up at the dark skies, remarking that he doubted very much if the fireworks display would be up to much on such a night.

A string of carriages lined the curb, the coachmen and footmen standing together in idle groups, some just talking, others more intent upon the turn of a card. Alabeth's skirts flapped as Charles handed her into his barouche, and the wind threatened to seize her bonnet from its pins and ribbons before Charles had climbed in too and the door was slammed.

Charles remained tactfully silent during the return journey, having realized that Alabeth's reason for leaving so suddenly had something to do with his revelation about Piers and Adelina. As she alighted at last outside the house in Berkeley Square, he took her hand, raising it gently to his lips. "Forgive me, Alabeth, I would not have said it for the world had I realized—"

"It wasn't your fault, Charles." She reached up to kiss his cheek and then was gone.

It was with some relief that she learned from Sanderson that Jillian was still asleep in her bed, for somehow she couldn't face the prospect of having a heart-to-heart talk tonight. She said very little to her maid as she undressed, and outside she could hear the gale howling around the eaves, rattling the windows, and making the curtains move as the draft found its stealthy way into the quiet bedroom.

The maid retired and Alabeth stood by the window for a while, looking out over the garden where the mulberry tree was swaying wildly to and fro and the flowers were bobbing, their colors muted by the darkness. In the distance, toward Chelsea, she saw the brief brilliance of some fireworks, but they were very few and after a minute or two there were no more.

She turned away, getting into the bed and curling up tightly, listening to the raging storm and trying to fend off the tears, but she could not. She hid her face in her pillow, weeping with all the agony of heartbreak.

25

She awoke the following morning to find that the summer storm was still raging. The gardens and rooftops were rain-washed, and low gray clouds sped swiftly across the heavens. Each gust of wind lashed the rain against the windows and the scene outside was distorted and indistinct —a world away from the glory of the previous morning. London was transformed from a dazzling, elegant city into a dismal, forlorn place where few ventured out.

As her maid dressed her hair, she listened to the wind moaning through the eaves and the tap-tapping of a branch of rambling rose against the windowpane. There was an unexpected chill in the air, making it seem more like January than July. She glanced at herself in the looking glass. There was rouge on her cheeks, but it did not disguise how pale she was. She felt very low, both because of Piers and because of having to confront Jillian about the rumors. All in all, it seemed set to be an odious day.

She turned to the maid. "How is Lady Jillian this morning?"

"Why, I don't know, my lady, for she hadn't stirred when I came up to you. Her maid was still waiting to hear from her."

Alabeth stared at the girl and then looked sharply at the clock on the mantelpiece. It was eleven o'clock and Jillian *still* hadn't risen? Something was wrong! Gathering her skirts, she hurried from the room, leaving her puzzled maid standing with the comb and pins.

Alabeth knocked on Jillian's door, but there was no reply. She knocked again, but still there was no sound from the room beyond. Taking a deep breath, she opened the door and stepped inside. It was still gloomy, for the curtains had not been drawn back, but as she crossed to the bed, she noticed incongruously that the doors of the immense wardrobe stood open. How careless of Jillian's maid not to have closed them. She drew back the floral silk hangings and looked down at the huddled shape in the bed.

"Jillian?"

There was only silence. Jillian did not stir at all at the sound of her voice.

"Jillian?" Hesitantly Alabeth reached down to touch the slumbering figure, but then her lips parted with horror, for the shape was far too soft and yielding. With a gasp she flung the coverlets aside and saw that beneath them there was only a large bolster. There was no sign of Jillian at all.

She felt ice-cold suddenly, staring at the bolster, her mind racing. Her trembling fingers crept to touch the ruff at the neckline of her gown, and she backed away from the bed. She heard her maid enter the room behind her and turned as the girl halted, seeing the bolster.

"Oh, my lady!"

"Have Sanderson come here immediately."

"Yes, my lady." The girl hurried away, so alarmed that she thought nothing of calling the butler's name as she went down the marble staircase. Her voice echoed loudly through the house.

Alabeth went to the wardrobe, looking hastily through the clothes. Jillian's traveling pelisse was gone, and several gowns, and her portmanteau was not in its place. Oh, Jillian, what have you done? She whirled about again as Sanderson almost ran into the room, still adjusting his half-tied cravat.

"You wished to see me, my lady?"

"Lady Jillian has gone. Have you any idea at all when?"

The butler looked completely dumbfounded. "Gone,

my lady? But we all thought she was still in her bed." His glance moved to the bolster.

"Go to the coach house—and quickly!"

He ran from the room again, and for the next five minutes Alabeth paced anxiously up and down, turning hopefully as he returned, but he shook his head. "No one knows anything, my lady. She didn't take a carriage."

"When was she last seen?"

"Her maid went to her room late last night, to close one of the windows because of the storm." He turned, beckoning to the white-faced maid, who stepped slowly forward.

Alabeth looked at her. "At what time was this?"

"Just before midnight, my lady."

"And you looked in the bed?"

"I saw only that she was huddled beneath the coverlets, my lady." The girl's lips were trembling and her eyes were huge.

Then Alabeth thought of something. "The wardrobe doors, were they open?"

"Oh, no, my lady. I'd have noticed if they were and I'd have closed them immediately."

So, Jillian had still been in her room at about midnight, but she could have crept from the house at any time since then. Where could she have gone? And what was worse, who was she with?

The servants watched her, obviously waiting for her commands, but she didn't know what to do, her mind was a complete blank. She couldn't think of what the right thing was; she didn't even know whom to turn to—except, perhaps, Octavia. "Sanderson, will you send a footman to Seaham House directly. I will write a note which must be handed to the Duchess."

At that moment there was a loud hammering at the front door, and hope surged into Alabeth's heart as she gathered her skirts, hurrying along the passageway and down the staircase, Jillian's name on her lips; but as the footman opened the door, it was a white-faced, anxious Charles Allister who stepped inside.

"Charles?"

He looked up swiftly, handing his dripping top hat and cloak to the footman. "Is Jillian here, Alabeth?"

"No."

"Then it's true—" He seemed suddenly quite overcome.

Alabeth was thoroughly alarmed, running down the last few steps to him. "Charles? What is it? What do you know?"

"She's run away with the Count; it's all over Town."

She stared at him. "Oh, no." Jillian was ruined forever, her character destroyed beyond redemption by this one rash, thoughtless act.

"I prayed it wasn't true," he went on, "for I did not think she could possibly be so blind."

"How is it all over Town?"

"The damned blackguard left a note pinned to the wall at Brooks's, callously informing the world that Lady Jillian Carstairs was running away with him and would become his mistress. There was no honorable mention of marriage, no thought at all of her, just the plain fact that she was going with him. What chance does she have with such a base creature? No *gentleman* would pen such a note, no *gentleman* would dream of even persuading a young lady into such an act, unless he had marriage in mind."

Alabeth could say nothing. The signs had all been there; she had seen them, but she had failed to act swiftly enough upon them. She had dithered, wanted to believe fibs; she had even allowed Jillian into the Count's company when she *knew* he was treacherous! As a guardian she had been an utter disaster; she had failed her father, failed Jillian, and she had failed herself! That she, the widow of Lord Manvers, could have been so utterly unguarded was beyond belief, for Jillian had followed the path she herself had taken all those years before—only for Jillian there was to be no haven of marriage, there was to be only ignominy.

Charles went to the fireplace at the side of the vestibule, resting one arm along the mantelpiece and staring down at the tapestry screen before it. "He isn't acting out of any love for her; he's obviously doing this simply and solely to strike back at me."

"At you?"

"Because I bruised his precious honor and mocked at his pride. He promised to have his revenge, and this is his way of doing it. How better to hurt me than by ruining the woman he knows I love? I wish to God I'd ignored Piers Castleton's interventions and had gone ahead with calling that Polish rat out."

Instinctively she went to him, slipping her hand into his. "The fault is equally mine, for I too bruised his pride when I spurned him. I even went to the length of striking his face when he became too importunate. He swore vengeance on me too. With one fell swoop he has hit back at both of us, but it is Jillian who will really suffer." Her voice shook a little. "Oh, Charles, what can we do?"

"There's nothing we *can* do, except sit tight and wait."

"But we can't do that."

"We have no choice, for we don't know where they've gone, do we? We will have to wait and pray that she returns safely."

"She's ruined forever, Charles." Tears filled Alabeth's eyes and she rested her head against his shoulder.

"Octavia says—"

"You've spoken to her?" Alabeth looked up immediately.

"Yes, she was on the point of leaving Town in some haste, as Seaham's mother has been taken very ill. I managed to tell her what had happened and she advised us to remain silent and just wait. She says that if Jillian returns and we don't appear to have acted with any real alarm, then we'll probably be able to brazen it all out and pretend it was a hoax. She says it's a slender chance; she realizes that, but she really doesn't think we have any other option."

Alabeth swallowed, for suddenly it seemed more hopeless than ever if Octavia was not close by to turn to. But Octavia's advice was common sense; it was their only hope, for if they could put a face on it, then maybe Jillian would not be completely ruined after all. Maybe.

Silence descended over the vestibule, broken only by the steady ticking of the long-case clock and the sound of the storm outside. A draft of chill air sucked down the chimney, making the bowl of flowers on the table tremble a little. Where was Jillian? What was happening to her at this very moment?

Alabeth was vaguely aware of the sound of a carriage halting outside and the coachman calling reassuringly to the restless, impatient team. She turned, and through the narrow glass beside the door she saw Piers Castleton's olive-green drag. Piers was alighting, the wind fluttering his cravat and the rain clearly visible on his light-gray coat. Just seeing him like that put a little courage into her, and she hurried to the door and out into the rain. "Piers?"

He turned toward her, smiling a little, and it was all too much for her. She ran to him, her eyes filled with tears, and he caught her close for a moment, his cheek resting against her hair. "I'll do all I can, I promise you," he said gently. "I came as soon as I received your note—"

Slowly she drew back. "My note? What note?"

He was startled by her reaction. "The note you sent to me about Jillian's disappearance."

"But I sent no note."

"Is it a hoax?" His eyes darkened a little.

"Would to God it was!" She bit her lip, turning away a little. The rain was soaking through her flimsy muslin gown and she shivered. The wind gusted along the pavement, whining through the plane trees in the center of the square and snatching bleakly at the wisps of smoke from the chimneys high above.

He removed his coat and put it gently around her shoulders. "Well, it doesn't matter about the note for the moment, it matters only that we find Jillian. Is there any news at all?"

"No." Her voice caught.

"Don't cry, please don't cry." He touched her cheek gently with his fingertips. "Come now, we'll go inside, for it will hardly be useful to have you wilting with an ague when we do find her."

She nodded tearfully, aware of his arm reassuringly around her shoulder as he walked her back toward the door of the house. "Piers?"

"Yes?"

"Thank you for coming."

"You should have thought of me straightaway. Indeed, I believed you had—"

His voice was so soft and tender in that moment that she could almost have confessed her love, but she remembered that he had asked Adelina to be his wife. He belonged to another now, and confessions were inappropriate. She drew away a little, and everything remained unsaid as she stepped into the vestibule where Charles was waiting anxiously.

"There is news, Piers?" he asked immediately.

"No, I'm afraid not." Piers tossed his top hat and gloves down upon the table next to the bowl of flowers. Damp marks were left on the highly polished surface. "Now, then, tell me all that you know."

Briefly they pieced together the portion of the jigsaw which they knew, and Alabeth was aware of how painfully little it was.

Piers listened in silence. "And you have no idea when she left the house?"

"Only that it was sometime after midnight." She shivered, still holding his coat close. It smelled of costmary.

"Well, I believe it almost certain that their destination will be France," said Piers thoughtfully, "for after his episode the Count will certainly be *persona non grata* in England, and his obvious course will be to return to Paris."

She was dismayed. "Then we can do nothing—"

"No? I think that is debatable, Alabeth. In this weather there won't be a single master who'll put willingly to sea, not even a French master, for someone like Zaleski. I'll warrant that every ship is still in port, waiting for calmer weather."

Hope began to brighten her eyes. Of course, the storm!

Piers went on. "Dover is the obvious place, for he entered England that way. It's my guess that they are there now, waiting to sail, and if I'm right, then we have an excellent chance of reaching them before they have a chance to leave for France. With your permission, Alabeth, I will go to Dover immediately."

Charles spoke up swiftly. "And I go with you, Piers."

"Naturally, I would not dream of excluding you. Alabeth, we will do all we can—"

"You do not imagine I am going to remain here on my own," she cried.

"Such a journey as this will hardly be a pleasure trip."

"I don't care, I am accompanying you. I refuse to remain behind."

He smiled a little at the indignant flash in her green eyes. "Very well, but one thing I do insist upon."

"And that is?"

"That you wear something a little more serviceable than muslin." He glanced down at the way her rain-dampened skirts clung to her legs.

She nodded, handing him back his coat and then hurrying away up the stairs, calling for her maid.

Piers turned then to Charles. "You do realize, don't you, that this may not turn out well, for even if we find them in Dover, Jillian may not wish to return with us."

"I know that." Charles lowered his eyes for a moment. "I love her, Piers, and I'm damned if I'm going to let her go with him. I'll *never* let her become anyone's mistress, least of all a man like Zaleski."

"I perceive that the Allister lamb is become something of a lion."

"And better late than never."

"Perhaps you are right." Piers looked up the staircase where Alabeth had been a moment before. "Yes, perhaps you are right."

26

The carriage traversed the well-paved streets of London swiftly enough, but the Dover road itself was quite another matter, being almost impassable in places because of the continuous downpour. Normally the journey to Dover could be accomplished in five hours, but today it would take a great deal longer.

From a hilltop south of the Thames, Alabeth looked back at the sprawl of the capital, the greatest city in the world, but half-hidden now beneath a pall of cloud and mist. Ahead lay Blackheath and the open road, once the route of pilgrims on their way to the shrine at Canterbury, but now frequently the haunt of highwaymen, especially on days such as this, when only a few dared to travel, for there were long periods when the road was quiet enough for them to do their evil work at leisure.

Piers continually scanned the countryside, and when he shifted his position once, Alabeth saw that he carried a pistol in readiness. A swift fear rose in her at this fresh danger, but it was a danger which must be faced if they were to reach Dover in time. She looked out at the horizon, afraid all the time that she would see a break in the clouds, heralding the end of the storm, but the clouds were continuous, the rain lashing against the glass. The grays hung their heads low as they battled against a wind which was more like a winter gale than a summer storm. The magnificent lacquerwork of the carriage was mud-stained, its color barely distinguishable now, and the horses were foam-flecked, their flanks steaming in the cold rush of wet air.

She huddled in a light-brown curricle cloak, beneath

which she wore an apple-green woolen gown. Apple-green was perhaps not practical, but then what lady of fashion possessed *practical* togs? Her bonnet lay discarded on the seat beside her, its pretty ribbons shaking to the motion of the carriage.

Ahead the road was a quagmire suddenly, a dip in the countryside catching the rain so that it lay in dangerously deceptive puddles which concealed the depth of the ruts beneath. The coachman urged the carriage slowly forward, the team planting their steps with care through the mire. The carriage lurched alarmingly and immediately Piers reached out to steady Alabeth, his fingers warm and firm around hers until the danger was past and the carriage was moving more easily again.

She wanted to cling to him, but knew that she must not. He glanced at her and saw the emotion in her eyes. He misinterpreted it. "We will reach her in time," he said gently and with more conviction than he actually possessed.

"I pray you are right," she whispered, looking out the window again. She could hear the Count's voice and see his face, made ugly by the twist of fury on his lips. "I swear that I will make you regret having played games. Before I have finished, you will wish with all your heart that you had accepted me."

After several hours, the weary team drew the carriage up at a posting inn, Piers knowing that their progress would be even slower unless the horses were either changed or at least rested. To her relief, there were fresh horses immediately available, and after taking some mulled wine, they were soon on their way again, the new team setting off at a handsome pace through the rain.

At last they were in sight of Dover, and the break in the clouds which she had been dreading was now visible on the distant horizon, spreading minute by minute until the sun was streaming through, turning the patch of sea beneath to a deep turquoise blue amid the gray. She watched it, her heart sinking, for already it was obvious that the storm was abating; the wind was less fierce and there were no longer rivulets of water streaming down the glass. How long would it be before the first ship set out for France?

Charles was dismayed too, sitting forward anxiously to lower the glass and urge the tired coachman to make more haste. The carriage began the descent into the old town, which nestled between steep chalk cliffs, on the northern one of which stood the proud old castle, facing resolutely out toward the coast of France, the hereditary enemy. The town crowded a sheltered gorge, the harbor and quay protected by the cliffs from the worst of the weather. A forest of masts and rigging swayed on the smooth water beyond the rooftops, and Alabeth looked at them as the carriage proceeded down the hill. Now that she was here, she knew instinctively that Piers had been right—Jillian *was* here somewhere!

Suddenly the wheels were rattling on firm cobbles again and the carriage moved much more easily. There were people hurrying along the pavements, and as Charles had left the glass lowered, they could hear all those sounds of a town which has just begun to emerge after a lengthy storm. Sparrows cheeped on the roofs and some dogs barked, a mother was scolding an excited child for jumping in an inviting puddle, and street vendors were calling their wares. High above, the patch of blue seemed to fill the sky now, and she could smell the perfume of mignonette from the pots in an open window as they passed.

For her those final minutes seemed like a lifetime. All she could think of was finding Jillian, and she prayed that she would be safe and well. So, when the carriage jerked to a sudden standstill because an ox cart blocked the way, she could have wept with frustration. But had it not been for that cart, she might never have glanced up at the windows of the small inn outside which they had halted, and she might never have caught that brief, brief glimpse of Jillian's pale, tearstained face peeping out.

Alabeth's heart almost stopped with shock, for the glimpse had been so fleeting that she thought she must have imagined it, but then the poor little face looked unhappily out once more and she knew beyond a doubt that it was Jillian!

"She's there, Piers," she cried, pointing up. "I saw her!"

He leaned forward immediately, following the angle of her finger, but there was nothing in the window now. "Are you sure?"

"Yes," she said, "yes, I'm sure."

He ordered the coachman to maneuver the carriage into the inn yard, and the hooves and wheels echoed beneath the low archway for a moment. The yard was ivy-clad and there was a gallery. A maid scuttled out, a bale of sheets clasped in her arms. She saw the carriage and hurried back inside again, calling to the innkeeper to hurry as there were gentry waiting to be greeted. In a moment the innkeeper appeared, hastily tying on a fresh apron and beaming all over his round face as he gestured to a tardy ostler to open the carriage doors.

Alabeth made to scramble swiftly down, but Piers restrained her. "You must remain here for the moment."

"But—"

"No, Alabeth, you stay here. Charles and I will find her."

"Please, Piers."

"It will be far from pleasant if we find the Count with her, and I would prefer you to be spared anything like that. Remain here and I will come for you."

Reluctantly she sat back, watching as he and Charles alighted. The door was slammed and she heard them inquiring of the startled innkeeper, who at first was unwilling to give any information concerning his guests, but who swiftly volunteered the necessary details at one cold glance from Piers' gray eyes.

The minutes seemed to trudge by as she waited. She toyed over and over again with the crumpled ribbons of her bonnet, twisting them around her fingers and gazing out all the while for sight of Piers.

He came at last, opening the carriage door and putting a reassuring hand over hers. "She's all right, Alabeth, a little tearful but quite all right."

She felt quite weak with relief. "He hasn't—I mean, she's—"

"He didn't touch her."

"Oh, thank God. He's with her now?"

"No, he's already gone to the quay. He had no intention of taking her with him, Alabeth. His intention was only to ruin her name, and this he believes he has done. Charles and I are going after him now."

Her eyes widened. "Please be careful." She remembered the pistol he was carrying.

Briefly his fingers brushed her cheek. "We will be careful."

He helped her down as Charles emerged from the inn, his face very pale and his eyes glinting with a deadly resolve. No one would be able to intervene this time should he find Count Adam Zaleski and corner him. He nodded curtly at Piers. "Shall we go then, sir?"

Piers nodded, and in a moment they were in the carriage, which was drawing back out into the busy street. Alabeth stood in the courtyard, listening until the sound of the carriage died away, and then she turned to the maid, who was waiting to escort her to Jillian.

27

Jillian was weeping inconsolably on the bed when Alabeth entered the little room, but hearing the light step, she sat up swiftly and then was running into her sister's arms. "Oh, Alabeth, Alabeth!"

Alabeth held her close, smoothing the tousled golden curls and whispering silly endearments. There were tears in her own eyes, tears of relief and tears of love for this most exasperating of creatures.

At last Jillian recovered a little, sniffing as she searched for another handkerchief. Alabeth gave her her own. With a small smile, Jillian took it. "I d-don't know wh-what to say," she said. "I f-feel so wretched and I've l-let you down so much."

"But you're all right, and that's all that really matters."

"I'm r-ruined, and we both know it. He l-laughed when he told m-me about the note he'd l-left at Brooks's." Jillian's eyes were a little haunted then, for the memory of that dreadful moment was so very hurtful, so very devastating. "I th-thought he was perfect, I thought he w-was the romantic lover I'd b-been dreaming of. I really b-believed him, Alabeth. I wouldn't h-have gone with him unless I had. I wanted it to be l-like you and Robert, I wanted that more than anything else in the world. B-but he only wanted to r-ruin me, h-he just wanted r-revenge."

"Oh, my poor darling."

"I should have l-listened to you, Alabeth, for you warned me about him."

"I know how persuasive he could be," said Alabeth, leading Jillian gently to the bed, making her sit down, and then she dipped a cloth into the bowl of cold water on the table and dabbed Jillian's tearstained face. "Don't cry anymore, for it's over now and we'll return to Town and carry on as before."

"I couldn't, I couldn't face them all."

"If we are sensible, then everyone will believe the note to have been a cruel hoax. You may not be ruined, my dearest, you must have hope of that. You don't imagine Piers or Charles will say anything, do you?"

A pathetic ray of hope sprang into Jillian's anxious eyes. "D-do you really think we could carry it off?"

"We have nothing to lose and everything to gain by trying."

"I've been such a fool, haven't I?"

"You've certainly been having a moment or two recently." Alabeth sat down next to her, taking her hands and squeezing them. Outside, the sun was still shining and she could hear doves cooing softly on the roof. In the distance the sea was sparkling and she wondered if Piers and Charles had reached the quay yet, if they had found the Count. Oh, please, God, keep them safe, keep them safe.

Jillian glanced at her. "I really admired your love for Robert, you know, I could not imagine ever settling for anything less. I thought about it all the time, dreaming romantic dreams and telling myself that I would be as fortunate as you were."

Alabeth lowered her eyes then. "Jillian, my life with Robert was not the wonderful dream it seemed to be."

"What do you mean?"

"I mean that although we began our life together very much in love, it was not the same by the time he died in that duel. He was a rake through and through, Jillian, and even though I think he still loved me, he continued to be a rake until the day he died."

"Surely not—"

"I knew that he gambled recklessly, but I did not know

how recklessly. He almost lost Charterleigh. He also kept a mistress."

Jillian looked quite stunned. "Oh, Alabeth!"

"So, you see, you were admiring something which was quite different from the way it seemed."

"I had no idea."

"I didn't exactly publish it all on a broadsheet."

"But you've never hinted that anything was wrong. I mean, ever since Robert died, you've been so loyal to his memory."

"I know."

"Why? Why didn't you tell me how it really was?"

"At the time it seemed the only way to be, but now— Well, now it's too late and the damage is done. In so many ways."

Jillian looked shrewdly at her. "You're talking about something else now, aren't you?"

"Yes."

"Tell me."

Alabeth stared at the window. "I remained loyal to Robert after his death because I felt unbearably guilty. Before he died, I had fallen in love with someone else, someone I believed to have been as responsible for his death as the man who opposed him in the duel."

Jillian stared then. "Piers Castleton?" she whispered.

"Yes."

"I don't know what to say." Jillian reddened, remembering her own fleeting infatuation for him.

"There's nothing to say, Jillian, for it's all to be forgotten now. He is going to marry Adelina Carver, and by my own actions over the years I've more than forfeited any chance of winning him. He wasn't responsible for Robert's behavior, I know that he wasn't, just as I now know the truth behind that duel he had with the Russian. There's so much that I know for certain now and that I accept, but it has all come too late. There is a moral in this

for you, Jillian Carstairs, for I believe that you feel far
more for Charles Allister than you've been admitting to
yourself. It may be too late for me, but it isn't too late for
you and Charles."

Jillian lowered her eyes. "Isn't it? Oh, Alabeth, he
won't want me now, not after this latest escapade."

"So, I'm right about your feelings for him?"

"Yes. I didn't really know it, though, until he walked
into this room a short while ago. In that moment I knew
how much I loved him. I suppose I knew it a little when
you wanted me to write to him, telling him that I didn't
wish him to pay court to me anymore. I wouldn't write
that letter because I couldn't bear to send him away. Oh, I
don't know what's been the matter with me, I *know* how
fine and good Charles is, I *know* that he would be the very
finest of husbands for me, but at the same time I couldn't
help yearning for someone with all the romance and excitement of a Robert or a Piers."

"Or a Count Zaleski?" Alabeth asked dryly.

"Well, I admit that that was an odious mistake, but he
looked so perfect."

"The flaws were there."

"Yes, I just didn't want to see them. Anyway, no matter
what you say about there still being time for me and
Charles, I think you are wrong. I am in the same boat as
you, Alabeth—between us we've bitched up our chances of
happiness."

"That is hardly a ladylike expression."

"It's how I feel."

Alabeth nodded. "Yes, I suppose I do too. But,
Jillian?"

"Yes?"

"I honestly believe that Charles loves you and wants you
still. I don't think he would have come here like this today
unless that were so. And you've admitted to me that you
love him, so *do* something about it! He may not be hand-

some and dashing, he may not cut the end of dashes all the time, but he's worth a thousand Count Zaleskis and a thousand Roberts. *Tell* him how you feel, don't leave it until it's too late, as I have done."

Jillian looked at her for a long, long while and then nodded. "I will do as you advise, but on one condition."

"And that is?"

"That you promise to do the same."

"It's too late, he's to marry Adelina now."

"It's *never* too late! She doesn't wear his ring yet, does she? You have to tell him how you feel, Alabeth, for if it's the right thing for me, then it's also the right thing for you."

"Oh, I don't know."

"Promise me, Alabeth."

Alabeth looked slowly into the bright-blue eyes and nodded. "Very well, I will tell him," she whispered.

Jillian's eyes fled toward the window and the sea beyond. "Pray God we aren't too late."

"Don't even begin to think it," said Alabeth sharply. "Don't even begin!"

They fell silent after that, each with her own thoughts and fears, and outside the street was so busy after the recent storm that they didn't hear the carriage returning; they knew nothing until Charles came into the room alone.

Jillian was on her feet in a moment. "Oh, you're safe," she cried. But Alabeth remained where she was, a dread creeping into her heart as she waited in vain for Piers to appear.

Charles saw the anxiety. "He's all right, Alabeth, he's down attending to the carriage."

Relief swept through her.

Jillian could not take her eyes from Charles. "Did-did you find the Count?"

"He was already on board a French packet which had put to sea. I wanted to pursue it, but Piers pointed out that no French master would heave to to hand over the First Consul's darling to a pair of revenge-seeking Englishmen." He smiled a little ruefully. "He was right, but I'd have given anything to get my hands on that filthy—"

Jillian took a hesitant step toward him. "It doesn't matter now," she said. "Nothing matters but that you are safe. Oh, Charles, I do love you so." Her large eyes filled with tears and she looked so appealing that no man on earth could have resisted. Her name on his lips, he went to her, holding her close, his fingers coiling in her short curly hair.

Alabeth slipped silently from the room, closing the door gently behind her. She paused for a moment in the low-ceilinged passage. Jillian had carried out her part of the promise, and her reward was that she was now safe and loved in Charles' arms. Now it was Alabeth's turn, but how could there possibly be such a happy ending for her? Taking a deep, trembling breath, she walked along the passage, gathering her apple-green skirts to descend the stairs toward the courtyard.

Piers was watching as a new team was brought for the return journey. He seemed to sense that she was there, for he turned, smiling, as he held out a hand to her. "I trust that all is well between Charles and Jillian."

"It is."

"Good."

"I'm so glad that you did not catch the Count."

"Perhaps it was just as well."

"Yes, I think so."

"He will not get away completely scot-free, for his reputation will suffer greatly as a result of what he did when he pinned that note to the wall at Brooks's. There is little chance of the tale not reaching Paris."

"I know."

He put his hand to her chin, raising her face a little.

"Don't look so despondent, for Jillian's character will survive, especially as she is bound to shortly become Lady Jillian Allister."

"We both have a great deal to thank you for, Piers."

"You should have written to me for help, you know," he said, "instead of leaving it to some unknown person to do that which should have sprung instantly to your mind." He took a piece of paper from his pocket and handed it to her.

She read it. "Piers. Please come to me, for Jillian has run away with the Count and I do not know what to do. Alabeth." She smiled a little, for it was Octavia's writing. Dear Octavia, remaining true to her promise to meddle if the situation should ever seem to warrant it.

"You recognize the writing?" he asked.

"Octavia Seaham."

"A very shrewd lady," he said softly.

"Yes. Piers?"

"Yes?"

She couldn't say it; the words were on the tip of her tongue but she couldn't say them. Once again all she could think of was that he had asked Adelina to marry him.

"What is it?" he asked.

"I want to wish you every happiness with Adelina."

He gave a short laugh. "Do you, indeed? I wonder what Harry Ponsonby would make of that?"

"I don't understand."

"Adelina is to marry Harry Ponsonby, so I doubt if I am about to enjoy any happiness with her at all."

"Oh." She felt totally bewildered.

"Alabeth, I once remarked to you that when I had last seen Adelina she had been looking triumphant and decidedly scheming, and I think that perhaps now is the time to explain it all to you. There was never a liaison between Adelina and myself; it was all a plot to bring Harry to his senses. Adelina is a dear friend, but I have never entertained any notion of marrying her. I pretended to court her in order to stir Harry's jealousy. The ploy worked admirably.''

"Oh.'' Her head seemed to be spinning. He wasn't marrying Adelina? He didn't love her?

He smiled at her. "Oh, Alabeth, does it not now occur to you that I had as much reason as Adelina to enter into the conspiracy?''

"You?''

"When sweet reason and patience failed, I had no other course than to try other means in order to prod you just a little.''

"Me?''

"Yes, you.'' His hand moved gently against her cheek and his eyes were very dark as he looked down at her. "That first time I met you, Alabeth, I had never in my life seen anyone more lovely, more enchanting, or more vulnerable. You were Robert's wife, so very young and only just beginning to see the unhappiness your notorious marriage was going to cause you. I wanted to rescue you, take you away from him, make you mine, and I could see in your eyes that you loved me too. Oh, you didn't want to love me, you felt disloyal—and I didn't want to love you, for you were another man's wife. I should have stayed away from Charterleigh, but I couldn't, for that would have meant not seeing you and I could not have endured that.''

"Oh, Piers,'' she whispered, tears filling her eyes.

"When he died, I hoped you would be mine, but instead you spurned me, indeed you seemed to hate me suddenly. I tried to accept that you would never be mine, and I thought I was beginning to get over you—until this spring, when you left Charterleigh and came to London again. Nothing had changed when first I saw you, Alabeth, I loved you still. I love you now.''

"As I love you,'' she said softly, "as I've always loved

you." The tears welled out of her eyes and down her cheeks. "Forgive me, Piers, forgive me for all I've said and done—"

"Forgive you? My darling, I *love* you." He pulled her close, kissing her on the lips. "There is nothing to forgive, for we've both said and done things we regret. It will all be different now, for you may have married the wrong man the first time, but you'll be marrying the right man this time."

He kissed her again, and she held him close, giving herself completely to the embrace. It was a first kiss, more heady and magnificent than any before, and all the sweeter for the years which had kept them apart. They were oblivious to everything, totally unaware of the astonished grooms and ostlers who watched them.

About the Author

Sandra Heath was born in 1944. As the daughter of an officer in the Royal Air Force, most of her life was spent traveling around to various European posts. She has lived and worked in both Holland and Germany.

The author now resides in Gloucester, England, together with her husband and young daughter, where all her spare time is spent writing. She is especially fond of exotic felines, and at one time or another, has owned each breed of cat.